The Feathery

For Janice
Bill Flynn

BILL FLYNN

THE FEATHERY

The Feathery

For Babushka
Courtney
Nathan
Hunter
Alex
Lily

ACKNOWLEDGEMENTS

Playing the great golf courses of Europe and attending several
British Opens with Norm Cullen, the real Malachy Gallagher and
Mike Tracy was an experience that aided in the making of this book...as
well as golf in the USA with my friends, Joe Ganem and the real Billy
McGinnis.
Kudos go to the professionals: Shannon Rothenburger Flynn, Donna
Lee Richards and Kate Heckman for taking a hard look at The
Feathery...and the responsive BookSurge team with Douglas Thompson,
Sarah Southerland and Julian Simmon.They all helped to smooth the
path to publication.

PROLOGUE

ST. ANDREWS, SCOTLAND

1849

A DAY SPENT WITH HUGH MCNAIR, FEATHERY BALL MAKER AND CHAMPION GOLFER

By Alistair Beddington, London Times
At
St. Andrews, Scotland, July 8th, 1849

A rain with wind came in the night. It rushed in from the Firth of Forth to sweep the Linksland. I knocked on the door just as a strong gust from the departing storm lashed at Hugh McNair's cedar-shingled cottage, turned gray by sea-salt and sun.

McNair opened the door straight away. I was surprised not to find a larger man. Perhaps his deeds on the golf course set my expectations. Instead, standing before me with an outstretched hand of welcome was a robust chap of around five-foot-seven inches. He was short necked with a black trimmed beard that was thicker on the sides than on the chin. McNair's pleasant face carried a Hibernian look resembling the Irish I'd seen on my trips to Dublin more than the features of Englishman or Scotsman for that matter. His build was quite compact except for a slight stoop to his shoulders. I found out later that that flaw in posture came from the force required to stuff feathers with an iron rod pushing hard against his shoulders when making feathery balls.

I introduced myself and confirmed my plan, sent earlier by post, to follow him before, during and after his match with Willie Dunn of Musselburgh. After greeting me he offered tea and poured. He placed his own mug on the window sill and bent low to look out at the Links of St. Andrews. I joined his search and saw dark clouds moving quickly across the morning sky.

Hugh raised a hand to his chin and stroked his beard, while saying, "If the wind doesn't die down by afternoon I'll need a heavier feathery ball for my match with Dunn." He took a sip of tea as he looked out at a treacherous part of the sixth hole rightly named The Lion's Mouth. It was a gaping sand-filled bunker with steep banked sides.

Hugh said, "a heavier ball would fly straight in a strong wind, but wouldn't gain enough distance to clear Lion's Mouth like a lighter feathery."

***

We left the cottage and started down a wagon path. It led us behind the first teeing place where several caddies were assembled. Some stood up from their lounging to shower Hugh with a chorus of respectful greetings. "Good morning, Sir." "Good morning, Mr. McNair."

Included in the group was Hugh's caddie. He introduced the lad to me as James McEwan. James was fourteen with tightly curled red hair and a face spotted with freckles. Hugh informed me that his father, Douglas, was a club maker and friend.

"It's a fresh morning, Sir, and ye'll be playing against Mr. Willie Dunn of Musselburgh," James said.

"Aye, lad, and ye'll be carrying me bag at mid-day when I do."

Whistles and other exclamations arose from the group. It was obvious they had a great deal of respect for the golfing ability and rivalry of McNair and Dunn...perhaps that rivalry extended to the golf ball-making trade.

"Mr. McNair, ye'll be playing your feathery ball today, won't ye," James McEwan blurted out, "whilst Mr. Dunn will play that hard lump of rubber gutty?"

Scowls by the other caddies burned in James' direction, followed by a slap on the head from the tweed cap of the older lad next to him. Hugh walked over and tousled his caddie's bright red hair. The other caddies grinned only after James' question seemed to gain the approval of his hero.

"Aye, I'll be playing with a feathery today," Hugh answered, "and always, until that gob of gutta-percha can fly better than it does now." Hugh took a club from one of them and swung it as if to make his point. "The Dunns of Musselburgh will play the gutty because they're set to market it."

Following Hugh's reply to young McEwan, Charles Dougal, a caddie the same age as Hugh at 43, spoke up. "I'll be using the gutty, cause the iron clubs rip and cut the leather if not struck well as your shots. I find the feathery too dear in price at two shillings when a gutty can be had for half."

Hugh gave Dougal a stern look. "I'll be playing the ball I make, Charles. That smooth gutta-percha ball doesn't fly and work as well in the air for me as a feathery."

Dougal nodded slowly. "True, but older gutties will fly as well as your feathery after they're marked by miss-hits."

Hugh's caddie, McEwan, spoke before Hugh could respond to Dougal's further endorsement of the gutty. "According to my notes," the McEwan lad said, "Mr. McNair will break his own record soon. He scored an eighty-one against Mr. Cowie of Montrose using his feathery ball."

A mixture of gasps and jeers came from the group for yet another outspoken remark from McEwan.

Hugh chuckled. "Thank you, lad."

It could've saved his caddie from another slap on the head from the same tweed cap.

***

On the way to his shop Hugh told me he'd taken James McEwan on as a caddie despite concern about his comments in front of other players. Hugh told me James was a good caddie, but then added that his eagerness and love for the game surmounted his sometime brazen behavior.

I followed Hugh into his shop nestled in among a row of small hotels and other businesses bordering the links of St. Andrews. He introduced me to Tom McIntyre as his partner in feathery ball making, and at times on the links during their golf matches.

Tom was busy stuffing goose feathers into a small hole in a piece of stitched leather using a crutch-handled steel rod. He held his shoulder up against the tool and moved it inward, guiding the tip with one hand and, with the other, providing feathers from a pocket that ran across his apron. Hugh mentioned that stuffing feathers was the critical step in making a good feathery. It would yield a ball with uniform hardness and shape, if done correctly.

Hugh went around his shop counting and touching the materials and tools used to make feathery balls. I tagged along behind. A bin was filled with goose down, and three large bull hides hung in one corner of the shop waiting to be worked by hand to soften them. He showed me some pieces cut to size and waiting to be sewn together as leather ball covers. One bull hide would supply enough leather for as many as 200 feathery balls…an amount sufficient for two months of production, at four balls per day. Hugh explained that the slow process accounted for the high price of a feathery, and the Dunn's gutta-percha balls requiring less cost for labor and material could be sold for less.

Two balls had been whetted in a solution of alum and water. They were drying on a shelf above the stove where the damp feathers would expand outward, and the leather cover would contract inward to give remarkable hardness to a ball stuffed with pillow-soft goose down. Next, three coats of paint would be applied.

Hugh weighed some finished feathery balls on a balance scale and inscribed their pennyweight on the painted leather covers. He explained that a pennyweight of 18.23 is equal to one ounce. The weight of each ball was controlled by a slight variation in thickness of the bull hide cover. The pennyweights ranged from twenty-six to thirty-two: a twenty-six pennyweight for calm air and a thirty-two pennyweight for a strong wind. Along side the pennyweight inscription on the cover the name, Hugh, was written there only when McNair decided a ball was proper to sell.

Hugh looked out on the links and seemed relieved to see no sign of a wind blowing there. He called McIntyre to his desk and asked him for a good 26 pennyweight feathery.

Tom went to a shelf above the stove and came back with a feathery. He told Hugh it was stuffed well and the stitching fine before handing it to him. Hugh gripped the ball and seemed satisfied with the feel before giving it to me. I felt the hardness, and tossed it up in the air a few times before running my fingers over the seams and returning the ball to Hugh. He picked up a quill and wrote HUGH above the pennyweight of 26 on the leather. When the ink dried he placed the ball in his vest pocket.

***

I arrived with Hugh McNair on the first teeing place of St. Andrews at noon. Willie Dunn was already there and dressed as Hugh was in a brown vested wool suit, leather necktie and tweed cap. Hugh's wicker club carrier was slung over McEwan's shoulder, and it contained seven clubs: a long-nosed driver, a long spoon, a middle spoon, a niblick, a cleek, a rut niblick and a green putter. Dunn's caddie held his man's same seven bunched under his arm.

It would be an 18-hole money match backed by Mr. Brown of Balgarvie at 200 pounds. Hugh would give Dunn a stroke on every 6th hole. He confided to me that three strokes was a lot to give Dunn, but it was a number dictated by the Society of St. Andrews Golfers.

His caddie reached into Hugh's wicker basket and pulled out a McEwan-made long-nose driving club. James ran his hand over the smooth blond thorn wood and seemed proud McNair would use a club made by his father.

"Ye'll put one past those Dunn gutty balls, Mr. McNair," the caddie said.

Hugh took the club in his hand and gave James a look he may have wished would quiet him on the tee. It didn't, and the caddie announced his golf ball theory.

"Mr. Dunn's smooth new gutty ball might fly farther later on if nicked by his miss-hits," Hugh's caddie said.

Dunn frowned and said, "would ye be keeping your lad quiet on the tee, Hugh?"

Hugh's smile turned to a look of concern. "I'll try to do that, Willie," he said.

The caddies told me a story about gutty balls. They'd said players not happy with newly purchased gutta-percha balls would give them to their caddies to whack around, and the more they were scarred, the better they flew.

The McEwan lad placed the feathery on a pinch of earth. Hugh took a practice swing with his stance wide over the ball and seemed to be looking at a church steeple target well beyond the links. His eyes went to the ball, and he placed the McEwan long-nose driving club behind it.

A smooth, deliberate swing of the driver brought the thorn wood head down to impact the ball. I heard a pleasant slap as the leather ball filled with feathers was met by the thorn wood driving club on the right spot. The bull hide must have compressed for an instant until the energy within the goose down recoiled, releasing the ball to flight. It flew from the tee on a high, climbing trajectory and soared upward and outward. The ball sustained lift for several seconds until gravity overcame the thrust of flight, and it dropped to the earth. It looked to be well over 200 yards from the tee. A loud cheer went up from the gallery.

Dunn's smooth gutty did not hold so long in the air and was propelled at least 25 yards behind Hugh's. It inspired only polite applause from the crowd.

After nine holes, the match was level at a score of 41 for both players. It was a different story on the final nine when McNair went five strokes up on Dunn with only two holes left.

Hugh was playing the best round of his life and kept it going at the 17th. When they reached the 18th tee, McEwan's smile was broad as if he knew his hero would exceed his own record score of 81. He placed the feathery on a pinch of sand and I was within earshot when he told Hugh, "some wind has come up behind ye back, knock yer feathery oot lang with this McEwan club, Mr. McNair."

He handed Hugh the thorn-wood driver. It was a solid drive. I paced it off to its resting place 240 yards straight down the fairway. I asked those St. Andrews men following the match if they'd seen any other drive go that distance. They all claimed it was the longest drive ever on the 18th. The feathery rested in a good lie for his second shot and, before Hugh could ask for it, his caddie pulled a long spoon out of the wicker carrier handing it to his player.

Hugh hit a perfect shot that bounced onto the 18th green where a crowd was waiting. Word spread to the avid golfers and golfing fans of St. Andrews that McNair was on the verge of a record, and they were on hand to bear witness to the miraculous event. All were hushed as he stood over his putt. Hugh stroked it well, and the ball dropped feather and leather silent into the hole for a 3, and a record score of 78 strokes. A loud roar went across the links and could've reached the center of St. Andrews. Those townspeople who hadn't made it to the match most likely knew what the cheer meant.

Hugh was congratulated by Dunn, whom he beat by six strokes. He hesitated before walking across the green to shake his caddie's hand, seemingly concerned on what might be said by James.

And his concern was well founded. The McEwan lad standing next to me said in a loud voice to Hugh, "did ye know Mr. Dunn broke his spoon club against the hardness of the gutty at the seventh?" Then the lad turned to me and said, "write that in your paper, sir."

I saw Willie Dunn's grimace.

Two men hoisted Hugh up on their shoulders to carry him to his shop. His caddie skipped blissfully along behind. The lads put Hugh down in front of his shop knowing he would join them later at the society's club room to take a drink from the Claret Jug, a tradition whenever a golfer from St. Andrews prevailed over one from Musselburgh.

I went with Hugh into his shop and to his desk. He took up a quill and inscribed his score of 78 below HUGH and the 26 pennyweight on the feathery. He placed the ball in a wooden box along with the record score card signed by the Secretary of the Society of St. Andrews Golfers. He slipped the cover into grooves on the box and slid it forward to closure.

His caddie was standing by the desk watching him mark the feathery. James McEwan still had the wicker basket of clubs slung over his shoulder.

Hugh withdrew the long-nosed driver Douglas McEwan made for him. With the same quill he wrote HUGH and 78 on the thorn wood head and handed it to James, saying, "Keep this club in the McEwan family, James, and don't be using it to poke down rabbit holes when hunting with your ferret."

It was the proper trophy to reward his caddie with on the record day I'd spent at St Andrews with Hugh McNair, a great champion.

SAN DIEGO, CALIFORNIA

2004

1

It was eight o'clock on an all-blue-sky Sunday morning. Zachary Beckman and his son, Scott, were getting ready to leave their custom colonial style home for a morning of golf. Diane Beckman entered the large country kitchen wearing a white silk robe. She was a woman who defied any disheveled, first thing in the morning appearance. Each of her real silver blond hairs had been combed in place. Her attractive face with high cheekbones held a bronze tennis court tan. Dianne's robe covered the hint of a well formed five-foot-nine inch body developed lithe and slender by spending most of her leisure time on that same court. Those features made her true age of thirty-eight seem years below that number. Her large blue eyes widened and then quickly narrowed to a squint before she spoke.

"Golf again, Zachary?" She angrily confronted her husband. "We're supposed to play a tennis match at ten with the Swansons. He's a large developer," she said, her voice reaching a high pitch, "and I need him."

"Sorry, Diane, but Scott has his heart set on golf with me today."

Diane turned in a white silk flourish and stormed out of the kitchen. Zachary told Scott to wait in the car then followed Diane upstairs toward their bedroom. He opened the same door that was slammed shut a few minutes before, and entered the large master bedroom with a four post bed and oriental rugs scattered in places to cover the polished oak flooring.

"No excuses or apologies, Zack. It's always golf, golf, golf. Damn golf. I hate it! And you spend all your spare time with Scott...none with me." Her voice was shrill, on the edge of a scream.

Zachary Beckman was only an inch taller than his wife at five-ten. His hair was black with a slight sprinkle of gray flecks hinting of more to come after his age of thirty-five. His face was not a classic handsome one, but was made rugged good looking by a broken nose not set properly after a rugby match. His body was toned, not only by golf and tennis, but by daily work-outs. His steel gray eyes expressed a marine pilot's intensity when he said, "there's a good excuse this time, Diane."

She looked at him through some tearing . "What might that be?"

"I was going to wait and tell you tonight when we were at the restaurant. But here goes." Zack took a deep breath. "I've volunteered to go to Iraq and I wanted to play golf once more with Scott before I left."

"Are you crazy? Iraq? Why?"

"The Marine Reserve trained me to fly helicopters in combat, and I've got to go."

Diane glared at her husband in disbelief. "You volunteered for this? When do you leave, and for how long?"

"This coming Tuesday, for a year, unless I'm extended."

She glowered at him in disbelief for ten seconds before she decided to take two steps forward toward the arms waiting to encircle her.

"Oh, Zach, I don't like this one bit. Please be careful. Don't make me a real widow instead of a golf widow."

Zachary Beckman laughed. "I'll make sure of that."

***

Later, when he was with his son on the 15th hole at Balboa, Zack told Scott about his going to Iraq.

Scott's eyes filled with tears. "How long, dad?"

"Should be home in a year."

Zachary stared at his son for a long time. Scott had the same silver blond hair and blue eyes as his mother But growing fast at twelve he'd be taller than her. His hair had started to meander down below the neck line...not Marine Corps length, but Zachary wouldn't rebuke Scott about his hair style, instead he took a digital camera out of his golf bag and said, "I'd like to take a picture with me of you swinging a golf club..."

Scott took his stance on the tee and swung a driver from his junior golf set while his dad clicked the camera several times.

When Zack finished taking the pictures, he looked into Scott's golf bag. "At the rate you're growing, you'll need an adult set of clubs next year. I'll buy you some when I get back."

CAMP VICTORY, IRAQ

2

Eleven months into his tour in Iraq, marine Captain Zachary Beckman was in the back seat, pilot's position, of an AH-1W Cobra attack-helicopter starting out on what he hoped would be one of his last missions before returning stateside. After the pre-flight activities, he looked at the snap-shot of his son, Scott, taped in a blank spot between several instruments on the fire-wall in front of him, and smiled.

As the Cobra lifted off, there was transmitted banter with his fire-control operator in the seat in front, about the mission and course to the target area. They flew low and fast over the desert for thirty minutes until the reported insurgent strong-hold was reached. They sighted their target. It consisted of two wood frame buildings. As Zachary started his pass to launch rockets at the buildings, all hell broke loose from both sides, front and rear. The helicopter started taking multiple hits from heavy caliber machine guns on the ground.

"It's a trap!" Zachary yelled, trying to bank the Cobra in a climbing, tight turn away from the ground-fire, but on that heading ran smack into two Stinger missiles shoulder launched by a pair of Iraqi bad guys. What happened next took place in fifteen seconds. The Cobra chopper started flying erratically because several hits severed a rotor blade and pierced some hydraulic control lines. Zachary tried, with the little control left, to make a hard-landing. But the Cobra was too low and moving too fast. The chopper hit the desert floor with a metal crunching impact followed by a ball of flame.

First to reach the burning helicopter was a thirteen-year-old Iraqi boy. The wreckage was still burning fiercely when he got there. He picked up a singed snapshot from the sand and studied it for a moment. It was a picture of a kid swinging a strange object. The boy shrugged his shoulders, tossed the photo away and sat down on the sand to wait for the wreckage to cool so he could search it for a much better prize.

SAN DIEGO

3

The rituals of the wake and funeral took on an unreal form for the late Captain Zachary Beckman's thirteen-year-old son, Scott. The funeral parlor lighting came mostly from four large candles above the closed casket. Burning wax combined with the floral offerings to fill the viewing room with a sickening sweet smell. Relatives, friends and a detail of marines glided slowly passed the casket. Scott and his mother greeted each and listened to their whispers of the proper funeral words. No tears came from Scott Beckman because his sorrow was frozen stoically in place.

***

Deep anger stayed with Scott at the graveside on a hill, under cloudy skies. Standing near a solitary palm tree, he watched his father's casket being slowly lowered into a dark rectangular hole. After the burial words from a rabbi, a marine officer in dress uniform handed Scott's mother a neatly folded American flag. As she took the flag in both hands, a group of Cobra helicopters flew below the clouds and low over the cemetery. A marine standing beside Scott bent down to explain a one-chopper gap in the formation. "That's a missing-man formation to honor your dad."

After weeks of holding back, tears started to escape…then Scott's anger exploded in a sobbing reply: "Lot of fucking good that does…he's dead."

He ran through the crowd around the graveside, shoving aside those mourners in his path, then lunged down a hillside, dodging gravestones on the way until he reached a line of parked cars along the roadside. He found his mother's Porsche and hit it with his fist. A bugler played taps, and that mournful sound was repeated by another horn in the distance. Shortly after the last note was played, Scott clenched his fist to punch the hood of the Porsche once again, but his mother came silently up behind and grabbed his arm with one hand and slapped his face with her black leather-gloved other one.

"You've embarrassed me in front of my friends and associates!" Diane Beckman screamed into Scott's tear-streamed face.

***

It was a Saturday thirteen months after the funeral. Scott was with his best friend, Matt Kemp, who'd lost his father in Iraq when a roadside bomb had detonated under his Humvee. They were hanging out at a strip mall making plans to shoplift a golf club that would be added to the old set they shared when trespassing on Balboa Country Club's 5th, 6th and 7th holes. Just before sunset they'd approach the course from a wooded area next to the fifth fairway. At twilight, there were seldom any players on those beginning holes to question their trespass. Scott and Matt called playing those three holes their *Balboa Loop*, and they continued to sneak on the course even after being caught, reported to the police and reprimanded.

The golf was fun, but the thrill of their law-scoffing transcended the playing of it. The cop that'd reprimanded them told the head-pro at Balboa that their trespassing was likely an outlet for the defiant anger over not having their fathers around to golf with. After knowing they'd both lost their fathers in Iraq, the head-pro at Balboa ignored their harmless twilight intrusions.

Now they were planning a more serious crime to join that same rebellious hostility.

"Are you sure we can pull it off this time?" Matt was slouched against the wall at a building across from an All in Sports store. "We blew it last time and got caught."

"That club was a driver, Matt. This one is going to be a wedge... much smaller to hide."

"It's still going to set off the metal detector at the front door."

"Yeah, but this time we don't stop...we run like hell."

They slowly approached the golf equipment section of the store, feigning a look at other merchandise along the way. When they reached the golf club display both picked up a club and wiggled it back and forth pretending to see how it felt. The club in Scott's hands was a 60-degree lob wedge. It was a club made popular by Phil Mickelson and Tiger Woods for hitting high shots to the green from close range. The price tag hanging on the wedge was $125.00.

***

Bill Tivey was sitting in the small security office with his feet propped on a table below three television monitors. Bill was in the Navy, stationed at Coronado, and he augmented his Navy pay by working security on weekends for All in Sports. Cameras scanning several areas in the store fed the TV monitors above him. It was a boring job, but he had the surveillance method down pat, switching his eyes from one monitor to another while reading a magazine and not missing any area scanned by the cameras. Very seldom did he have to pick up his radio from the table and alert the front door security guy that someone was trying to vamoose with shop-lifted goods.

Tivey's eyes went to the middle monitor. It was displaying the view from a camera in golf goods, and it caught a kid stuffing a golf club down the pant leg of his baggy shorts. He watched the kid cover the top of the club with his loose fitting sweatshirt. The monitor showed another kid dressed in the same over sized clothes standing close by, acting as a lookout.

He grabbed his radio from the table to alert the security guy posted at the exit. "Bingo, in sporting goods," said Tivey. "A kid in shorts and sweatshirt just lifted a golf club. There's another kid with him."

He was quickly out of his office and on the run. Tivey, with the front door guard, caught up to the boys and grabbed them as they were making a dash to escape through the main exit. They held the boys firmly by the arms and escorted them to the security office.

"That's a stupid thing you did," said Tivey. "We have it all on videotape."

Scott pulled the lob wedge from his shorts and sweatshirt placing it on the table. "We didn't know you had TV. Last time it was just a metal detector."

"Yeah, you were caught on *Candid Camera.*" Then Tivey said, "okay, I have to make a phone call to the San Diego police dispatcher." He took a deep breath and paused before asking the question that always saddened him. Bill Tivey didn't like this part of his job, but the answer he got from Scott made it worse than ever. "Do you want to call your fathers so they'll be here when the police arrive?"

Scott answered for the both of them. "They're dead. Killed in Iraq."

Those words from Scott shook Tivey. He mumbled something about being sorry. And then he made a decision to call Detective Ross instead of the police dispatcher. He thought Ross might keep these two kids away from more trouble.

4

Detective Kyle Ross of the San Diego Juvenile Unit picked the boys up at the store and drove to downtown San Diego where he'd meet with Mrs. Beckman, Scott's mother.

Ross was forty-four years old, a rugged six-foot-three African-American who'd stayed in shape after playing linebacker for San Diego City College and that same position for the Cherry Point Marine team. He had a full head of premature gray hair that was a handsome contrast to his ebony skin color. After the Marine Corps he became a cop and spent his first years in law enforcement in the homicide division before being transferred to Juvenile. Juvenile turned out to be his calling. Ross helped keep kids from going to jail before that penal system educated them into committing more serious crimes. Ross waited impatiently for fifteen minutes before Mrs. Beckman gave the okay for her secretary to usher him into her office. She made a half-hearted apology about being tied up with a client who was about to close on a twenty million dollar property. Diane Beckman was the president of one of the largest real estate companies in California. She had movie star looks. To Ross her makeup appeared as if it'd been applied professionally, and her hair most likely styled weekly. His experience in Juvenile dealing with rich parents told him this woman fit the profile of one whose ambition to succeed in business transcended good parenting.

"What now?" Diane Beckman asked.

"Your son, Scott, was caught shoplifting again."

"Oh shit. Where this time?"

"At All in Sports. Security there caught him on their surveillance video camera trying to stuff a golf club down his pant leg. He was with another kid...Matt Kemp."

"Great, last time it was a big golf club. Matt was with him then, also."

"Yeah, that time it was a driver, Mrs. Beckman. Today it was a lob wedge."

"Whatever." She shrugged her shoulders. "I know very little about golf clubs. Where's Scott now?"

"All in Sports didn't press charges, and both kids are waiting in my vehicle. They're sweating out what's going to happen to them next. I'd like to talk you about those options."

Diane Beckman anxiously looked at her watch. "Okay, but I've a very important meeting in ten minutes."

Ross gave her a hard stare. "This is about your son, Mrs. Beckman."

"I know, but there's nothing I can do to change him. He's just like his father. Scott's obsessed with golf like Zachary was." She shrugged her shoulders again. "He'll probably end up spending all his time golfing just like his father did."

"What do you think is going on with your son to make him disobey the law?"

"He loved his father and is still angry about losing him. He won't accept my attempts to take charge of things. Scott hardly ever talks to me."

"Besides that...what's this thing with his stealing golf clubs about?"

"My husband started Scott into golf before he was called up by the Marine Reserve. He'd taken Scott out to the Balboa Course many times. They'd played that course together, and Scott fell in love with the game. By the way, detective, I hate golf." She paused and seemed to be thinking about how to tell the rest. "His dad was going to buy Scott a set of clubs for his thirteenth birthday when he got back from Iraq." There was another pause. "I was against it. I wanted Scott to concentrate on tennis."

"And what else?" Ross prodded her to go on.

"I gave all of my husband's things to the Salvation Army the day I got notified of Zachary's death. Maybe it was a crazy thing to do, but I wanted nothing left in the house to remind me of him. And throwing out everything of his helped me work off some anger. You see, detective... Zachary did not have to go to Iraq...he volunteered, of all things."

After that statement, Ross' opinion of this career-bent, self-centered woman degraded even more. He thought about the 214 Marines from Camp Pendleton, close by San Diego, who'd been killed in Iraq. His loyalty to the corps hit home, and the motto *semper fi* came to mind before…"I suppose your husband's golf clubs went with the other stuff."

"Yes, especially the golf clubs and his golf balls, golf books. Yes, even his golf shoes and clothes. It's been over a year since, and Scott hasn't forgiven me for throwing those golf things out."

"After you tossed out his father's clubs, couldn't you buy Scott his own set?"

"No, I refused to let him get involved in the game of golf. Tennis, in my opinion, reaches a higher quality of clientèle, and it takes less time away from business to play. Scott still refuses to take tennis lessons, and I'll not let him take golf lessons or be involved with golf." She looked at her wristwatch again.

"Well, that takes a lot away from the purpose of my visit."

"What do you mean, Detective?"

"I came here to ask your permission to have your son join a program run by a golf pro at El Camino. He's helped other kids in trouble by keeping them busy at the golf course."

"Golf…no way, detective."

Ross stood up, and glared down at her. "Look, Mrs. Beckman, your son has committed a crime. I can take him down to juvenile court and book him or out to El Camino. It's your choice."

Diane Beckman's eyes went again to her wrist. "Do they have a tennis program at El Camino?"

Her rude time-checking was irritating Ross. "I suppose they do."

"Well, I don't like this, but you haven't given me a good alternative. You may take Scott out to El Camino, only he should play tennis there. Now, I really must go to my meeting, detective."

"Thank you for your time, Mrs. Beckman. I'll take Scott out to El Camino today." Ross thought she'd hurriedly made her decision based on the time for her meeting and a tennis program at El Camino for her son instead of golf.

***

In the backseat of Ross' unmarked police car the two boys sat wondering about their fate. To make sure they didn't run, and for effect, Ross had handcuffed Matt's right hand to Scott's left. Scott's right wrist was connected by another set of cuffs to a handhold in the vehicle. The good-looking fourteen-year-olds were scared. Scott was the tallest at five-feet-seven, and Matt was a couple of inches shorter. Their oversize shorts and sweatshirts hung down below their knees. Scott was a blond with straight white teeth. Matt's hair was dark red. He had a few freckles and two front teeth that needed to be pulled back in line by an orthodontic procedure. Their hair was long, in need of a good shampoo, and their baseball caps turned backwards didn't hide that unkempt state. They watched Detective Ross walk toward them across the black asphalt parking lot next to Mrs. Beckman's office.

"Jeez, here he comes." Scott's heart started beating faster. "My mother doesn't give a shit if I go to jail."

Matt turned his head to watch Ross' approach. He self-consciously covered his two protruding teeth with his upper lip. "Mine doesn't either."

Detective Ross didn't get in the driver's seat right away. He went to the open rear window to ask Matt for his mother's phone number.

"She's not home; she's in Crawford, Texas. Travels all over the country protesting the war in Iraq. My grandmother's at my house." He gave Ross the phone number.

Detective Ross moved away from the car, out of earshot. He called the number to brief Matt's grandmother and ask her permission to take Matt out to El Camino Country Club. He got the permission and placed another call to the head pro at El Camino, Sandy McNair, to tell him he was on the way there with two more troubled kids.

Ross was silent as he drove out of the parking lot. It surprised the boys in the back when the detective headed away from downtown San Diego on the freeway. They expected to be taken to Juvenile Hall.

Scott got up the courage to ask: "Where are you taking us, sir?"

"To San Quentin..." Ross paused for effect. "No, we're going to El Camino Country Club. I want you both to meet a man who may help you stay out of San Quentin or any other jail."

As he drove toward El Camino, Detective Ross formulated the lecture he would give to the boys before they met Sandy McNair. After a short drive he got off the freeway and continued on for less than a mile before turning into a roadway lined with palm trees. It led to the El Camino clubhouse parking lot. He pulled into an empty spot, shut off the engine, and turned around to face the boys in the back.

Ross' eyes shifted slowly from Scott to Matt before he spoke. "Okay, here's the deal. You guys are headed from petty theft to more serious crime unless some changes are made. You're going to have to work on those changes, and you'll need help to get it done. Do you both want to hear about a program at El Camino that could improve your attitude?"

Scott and Matt looked at each other for a moment and then both nodded.

"I'm going to introduce you both to Sandy McNair in a few minutes. He's helped kids turn it around. Sandy is going to keep you busy at the golf course and out of trouble. You must report here at El Camino after school and on weekends. Do you both go along with that plan?"

Scott agreed readily, "Okay." He looked over at Matt, but there wasn't a response to Ross' question from him.

A nudge from Scott's elbow produced a delayed answer from Matt... "Yeah, guess it could work."

One of Ross' eyebrows raised, and he stared at Matt for ten seconds before he asked. "Any questions?"

"Do we get paid, and can we play golf?" It was Scott who asked that question.

"Yes, it'll be a variety of jobs at minimum wage and some work as caddies. As far as golf is concerned...that'll be up to Sandy."

Scott smiled for the first time in a while and said, "cool."

Detective Ross paused for a moment before he spoke again. "Let me tell you a little about Sandy McNair. He's eighty-five-years-old, and according to *Golf Digest* magazine he is rated as one of the top-ten golf instructors in United States. Sandy was a thirty-year-old assistant pro at Saint Andrews, Scotland, when his wife and two-year-old son were killed in a vehicle accident. Anger about their loss consumed him. Sandy's surroundings at Saint Andrews were haunting him, so he left there for the United States. He focused on teaching golf here, and gradually the anger left." Ross had their attention, so he asked, "Do you know why I'm telling you guys about Sandy?"

"Because we're both pissed off about our dads being killed like Mr. McNair was about his wife and kid." Scott's eyes filled with tears as he said that, and the same was happening to his friend seated next to him...tears were a rare occurrence for both boys.

"Right on," said Ross. "The anger is making you defiant. It's causing you guys to steal and trespass on a golf course. It's up to you to work with Sandy and turn it around." He stared both of them down before he asked the key question, "Are you ready to give it a shot?"

Scott nodded in agreement, and it took another elbow nudge from him before Matt slowly indicated his okay.

"All right. Then let's go meet Sandy McNair."

***

They passed by several golfers stroking putts on the practice green while waiting to be called to the first tee. Two of them greeted Ross with respect. Ross was the first African American man to become a member at El Camino, and Sandy was the one who convinced the board of directors to let him in. Others followed, and two years after joining El Camino, Ross became the club champion.

Ross, with the two boys following him, entered the clubhouse and walked toward the counter, passing by displays chock-full of golf clubs and clothing. An assistant-pro told Ross that Sandy was waiting for them in his office.

Ross knocked once, and they heard a brusque voice in response, "Come on in."

Sandy's tone made Scott wonder if they were about to meet *a tough, kick ass and take names* kinda guy…That expression came from some marine-speak he'd heard from his father.

They entered the office. The walls were covered with framed photographs. One was of Arnold Palmer. Others were of Jack Nicklaus and Ben Crenshaw. In the photos, they were standing next to Sandy. The much older Sandy got up from a chair behind his desk and approached them slowly like his eighty-five year old joints were stiff from sitting. Sandy was dressed in old-fashioned golf attire: a leather necktie, a Harris Tweed jacket with elbow patches and red plaid plus-four knickers like the boys had seen worn by the late-great Payne Stewart.

Sandy stuck out his right hand to them, and he smiled. Sandy's face was wrinkled and browned from his many years in the sun, playing and teaching golf. His hair was mostly white with a few strands that hinted at the red color it had been in his youth. He greeted Detective Ross with a wink. "Are these the two lads that need a lob wedge? We have a few of those around here." He shook Scott's hand first and then Matt's.

Scott recalled his dad teaching him the correct grip on a golf club. *'Soft...like holding two baby birds'*, he'd said. Sandy McNair's handshake was like that...soft, but not limp or wimpy. Scott noticed that the blue in Sandy's eyes was clear, not clouded or milky like some old men's.

Sandy's eyes shifted to all three of them. "I haven't taken lunch." Sandy said. "How about joining me?" He looked directly at both boys. "They make a great cheeseburger with fries at our Hole 19 Lounge."

The distress of their day had masked their hunger until the mention of their favorite food brought it quickly to the surface.

Sandy put a hand on each of their shoulders, and they headed out the door of his office and down a hallway toward the restaurant. His hands resting on their shoulders were not only a gesture of acceptance and welcome, but helped to steady his stiff, arthritic gait.

"I'll bow out of lunch. I'm going to hit a few balls on the range." Detective Ross said, "catch you later." After saying that, Ross turned in the opposite direction and walked down the corridor toward the pro shop.

The table reserved for Sandy overlooked the 18th and the practice green. As they sat down, a foursome was making their approach shots to the 18th green.

Sandy broke the ice. "See that player in the red shirt who's about to make his chip shot from ten feet off the green?"

Both boys zeroed in on him.

"Most likely he's chipping for an eagle on that 542 yard, par five."

They watched as he made the shot. The ball rolled straight to the cup and stopped an inch away from dropping in. The golfer walked up to the ball and tapped it in for a birdie four...if Sandy's guess was correct.

"That's Ray Billings. He owns Billings Manufacturing. They manufacture auto parts and are a Fortune Five-Hundred company. Detective Ross brought him to me when he was sixteen after he got in trouble stealing cars and stripping them for parts. He went to work here. We taught him to play golf and handle life. There were many others that got the same help at El Camino. Some went on to bigger-better things. We tried with some others, but they never made it."

The boys were silent as they watched Ray Billings shake hands with the other members of his foursome and make his way off the green. As he passed by the window next to Sandy's table, Billings waved before gesturing with both thumbs held high. Sandy smiled and waved back.

Sandy leaned forward, folded his arms and placed them on the table. His clear blue eyes narrowed. "Okay lads, let's cut to the chase. I'm here to help you. Tell me what's going on."

They opened up and told Sandy about losing their fathers. They both agreed when he surmised that those feelings caused them to rebel and to flout the law by stealing. Scott started to trust the wisdom of this old man sitting across from them who talked softly and held their attention with his bright eyes peering straight at theirs. It also helped for them to know he had suffered from a loss like their own.

Their cheeseburgers and fries with cokes arrived at the table. They all ate in silence, looking out at the golf course. After they finished, Sandy laid down the rules.

"Okay, I know about anger like that. I lost my wife and young son years ago. It took me a long time to get over the rage, but dedicating myself to teaching golf helped me do that. You have to get away from the anger by committing yourselves to a worthwhile activity instead of getting in the kind of trouble you've been in. Do you both want to work here and learn about golf?"

Scott immediately answered in the affirmative. There was a delay of five seconds before a stare from Sandy caused Matt to say, "okay."

Scott asked his first question. "What will we do?"

Sandy noted Matt's reluctance to show any enthusiasm and thought he should be turned over to Harry Gladstone who had a way with the hard ones. "Many different jobs…I'm going to split you up. Matt, you'll work with our greens keeper at first. He'll keep you busy, and I want you to know every part of the course before you start to caddie for the caddie master, Billy McGinnis." Sandy shifted those clear blue eyes toward Scott. "Scott, at first, you'll stay with me on the range when I give lessons. The arthritis in my joints is getting worse and I need help there. Later on, you'll be working for the caddie master doing loops for our members."

"Will you teach us golf?" Scott asked, "and can we play the course?"

"I plan to give you lessons. You'll play the course every Monday when I think you've learned the game and improved your attitude. This includes keeping up in schoolwork and not getting in the kind of trouble that brought you here. Do you both agree with my plan?" Sandy peered from one to the other waiting for an answer.

Scott said, "yes sir."

Matt hesitated again before he answered with "yeah."

"Okay. Tomorrow is Sunday. Be here at eight sharp." Sandy paused to look up and down at their over sized shorts and sweatshirts. "And, lads, in the morning, I'd like to see those Padres baseball caps turned around so the visors are in front instead of in the back. Also, those shorts and shirts you're wearing are at least three sizes too large. On your way out, pick up some in the pro shop that fit you and charge them to me. As far as the hair is concerned, you can keep it long, but please wash it."

They were on their way to the driving range to meet Detective Ross when Matt protested, "Jeez, Scott, this sucks. I don't know if I'm ready to get decked out in tight clothes, turn my hat around and become a frigging fag overnight."

Scott stopped walking and grabbed Matt by the arm. "So, you'd rather get busted, asshole? And by the way, I was onto your act taking so long to agree when asked by Ross and Sandy if you'd go along with the program."

"Yeah, I could feel your fucking elbow."

"What's your problem, Matt?"

"I'm not sure I want to be told how to dress and get tied down working on a golf course. It takes too much time away from surfing and my rap music."

"Best that you give it a shot. It's better than jail, and you'll still have time to take on that weird combo of rapper and surfer."

***

Detective Ross drove into the Beckman circular driveway and let Scott out in front of the huge colonial style house with a tennis court beside it that covered an area twice as big as Ross' own back yard. *To support a place like this*, he thought, *Mrs. Beckman has to sell hell of a lot of real estate.*

Ross turned around to speak to the boys in back. "Good luck at El Camino. I'll be checking up on you from time to time. By the way, you might mention something to your mother, Scott, about the tennis program there. It'll make things at home go a lot smoother for you."

"Yeah, she's trying to push me into tennis. Hates golf. Gave my dad a hard time about playing it." Scott stood before Ross' open window a few seconds. "Thanks, Detective Ross." He reached through the car window to shake Ross' hand and felt the firm grip of Ross' large one not ready to release his own.

Ross increased the pressure to make sure he had Scott's attention. "Your mother is still going to give you a hard time about golf. She has a thing about it, so you may have to pick up a tennis racket once in a while at El Camino."

"I understand." Scott looked at Matt in the back seat and spoke to his friend saying, "Later."

Matt scowled back at him.

Ross watched Scott walk up the steps to his front door. His baseball cap was turned around so the visor was in front. Ross glanced in the backseat. Matt's cap was still on backwards.

5

Sandy McNair was awake at six in the morning. He prepared his breakfast in the little kitchen of his one bedroom apartment above the El Camino clubhouse. Sandy had lived alone ever since the tragic of loss of his family. On this morning, he looked forward to the challenge of turning the lives of two more kids away from trouble.

His gut feeling was that Scott would make progress at El Camino to shed the anger and resulting defiance brought on by the death of his father. He'd detected a harder, more unwilling attitude in Matt. But the greens keeper, Harry Gladstone, could work on that. This morning he'd turn Matt over to Harry.

During his meeting with the boys he'd observed that Scott was keen to start learning golf. Years of experience in the game suggested to him that Scott had the build and the hands to be a player. He would work with him to lay down some good fundamentals as a start.

Sandy sipped on his breakfast tea and looked around his small apartment. Golf antiques and memorabilia were placed on shelves in a maple cabinet. The items originated from St. Andrews in the 1800s and were handed down to him through generations of McNairs. The McNairs of that era in St. Andrews were golf ball and golf club makers. They'd also excelled at the game of golf.

He opened the glass door of the cabinet and removed a small wooden box. He slid back the cover and stared admiringly at his most prized possession inside. It was an antique golf ball called the feathery. It had a leather cover and was stuffed with goose feathers from the shop of his great grandfather, Hugh McNair. Hugh had used this same feathery ball when he set the course record score of 78 at St. Andrews in 1849. Another glass case held Sandy's trophies won in golf tournaments during his younger days at St. Andrews. The name on each trophy was *"Alan McNair"* instead of Sandy. His nickname came from once being a sand-colored redhead and it stuck with him through the years, even after his hair had turned almost white as snow.

Every morning before he left the apartment to go downstairs he'd glance at a black and white framed photo of his wife and two-year-old son. A flash of anger would find him. Then it would quickly subside when his mind switched to the golf lessons scheduled or a troubled kid in need of his help. On this morning, he'd initiate an attempt to guide two more lads away from their wrath and toward the serenity of a purposeful life.

***

Sandy joined Scott and Matt in the pro shop. Their new shorts and shirts were a much better fit than the baggy clothes they had been wearing yesterday. But Matt's hat was still turned around with the visor in the back. Both boys had recently shampooed their long hair.

They followed Sandy to the Hole 19 Lounge. They had coffee and Danish and met some of the El Camino staff who were on break. Included in the group was the greens keeper, Harry Gladstone, and the caddie master, Billy McGinnis. Billy was a disciplinarian like Harry and Sandy planned to turn Matt over to Billy at some point. Matt left with Gladstone, and Scott followed Sandy to the practice range.

Scott's first job was to fill the golf ball buckets used for lessons and run errands from the range. In general he became Sandy's *gofor*. Scott watched as McNair taught golf and took in his instruction of proper setup and tempo. At times, gruff words provoked by the ache of arthritic joints in his aging body would overcome Sandy's usually patient teaching disposition. He'd vent the anger caused by his pain by yelling at his students when their alignment was off, "Keep your damn ass behind you!"

Some players from the tour came to El Camino to have Sandy take a look at their swing. He'd introduce Scott to them, and it was a thrill for him to watch these pros hit balls while listening to their banter about the PGA tour. Between lessons, Sandy spent time with Scott, schooling him on the proper swing dynamics. From his years of experience in the game, Sandy recognized Scott's natural ability and took on the project of nurturing it. Scott was a zealous student, eager to learn. He practiced golf for hours while making only token appearances on the tennis court.

Gladstone, the greens keeper, was tough on Matt at first and assigned the hardest jobs to him, like hours in the hot sun sifting sand for bunkers. The first week Matt was on the verge of quitting, and had a talk with Scott about doing so.

"Jeez, Scott, it's like boot camp. Gladstone is like a frigging marine drill instructor."

"Hang in, Matt. Look how tan and shaped up you're getting. You'll look great on a surf board."

***

After three months Scott was rewarded for his work and attitude turnaround by being allowed to play the course on Monday afternoons. Because those front teeth protruded over his lower lip Matt was called, Bucky Pearl, by the caddies and wasn't allowed to join Scott on Mondays after he'd had a fight with the caddie who'd nicknamed him that. Anyway, Matt didn't have the fervor for golf to match Scott's, so his punishment wasn't a severe one.

Scott practiced and played whenever he wasn't working or caddying, Caddying helped to teach both boys proper conduct on a golf course and instilled the discipline so lacking in their fatherless up-bringing. But it was Matt who continued to excel at caddying, and after a year, he became the most sought-after looper at El Camino Country Club. Detective Ross checked in on them from time to time and was pleased with their progress.

***

By the time Scott was a junior in high school, the arthritis had worsened so severely in Sandy's hips, that he required an operation to replace both hip joints. In the morning, before school, Scott would help him get from his apartment to his wheelchair and to the range for his lessons. Sandy could still teach golf sitting in the wheelchair. He continued to observe the student's golf swing with those clear blue eyes focused on every move, and if he detected a swing flaw he'd coach it to correction with a few words of instruction.

Meanwhile, it was golf course maintenance and pro shop duties for Scott. Matt still maintained his zest for caddying and started working some amateur tournaments around the San Diego area. On days he wasn't caddying he could be found satisfying his other two passions...surfing on some of the best waves colliding with one of the many San Diego beaches or attending rap concerts. But for Scott it was golf and golf only, and his token tennis sessions dwindled down to none. Throughout his teenage years, Scott did well in amateur competition under Sandy's tutoring, but his mother refused to watch him play.

***

During Scott's senior year of high school, Pepperdine University offered him a full golf scholarship, and he eagerly accepted it as a stepping stone to the PGA Tour. Matt's being teased about his protruding front teeth caused more than one fight, until Sandy paid an orthodontist to bring them in line. When Matt graduated from high school with no desire to attend college, Sandy used his connections to get him a job as a caddie on the Nationwide Tour.

They worked their last summer together at El Camino. It was the end of August when Scott and Matt were on the practice green putting for quarters. A 21-foot putt by Scott snaked its way to the hole and dropped in. Scott loudly proclaimed victory: "I've won the Masters. The green jacket is all mine!"

Scott's habit of inventing a major tournament's final day and final putt stayed with him since he'd first held a putter. He wanted to bring that form of intense concentration with him when stroking putts on the greens of competitive golf.

"Hey, dude, that's enough. Take my quarter and quit pretending you're at Augusta," Matt said, as he tossed the coin to his friend.

Scott put his hand on Matt's shoulder as they walked off the practice green and said, "some day, buddy, it's gonna be Augusta for real."

Matt's smile offered a rare glimpse of teeth bound with silver wires."And when it is, I'll be on your bag."

At his table overlooking the practice green, Sandy watched as Scott's long putt dropped in the cup. A wide grin came to his weathered face as he recalled the day Detective Ross had brought the lads to El Camino. He waited at the table for both boys to arrive for their going-away dinner. He had their names engraved on two golf clubs as going-away gifts. The golf clubs were leaning on a chair next to him...they were 60-degree lob wedges.

They were enjoying a meal of steak, salad and French fries when, out of the corner of his eye, Scott saw his mother rushing toward the table with her tennis-pro-boyfriend trailing meekly behind her.

Diane Beckman screamed at Scott: "You think I don't know you've spent all your time out here learning golf instead of tennis. You're just like your father was. Golf, golf, golf and more golf."

Scott was embarrassed. Sandy started to rise, but sat back down when she continued her tirade.

"Now I understand you'll play golf at Pepperdine. You'd better have a good scholarship because you will not receive one red cent from me while you're there."

She spun around and left the table, followed by the tennis pro, before Scott or anyone else could say a word.

SANTA BARBARA
&
THE MONTEREY PENINSULA
CALIFORNIA

6

A DECEMBER AFTERNOON FIVE YEARS LATER

Welcome to Santa Barbara, Dude...long time no see." Matt Kemp reached into the cooler and handed Scott a can of Coors. "Are we ready for the Q?"

Scott had driven from San Diego to Matt's condominium high up in the hills above Santa Barbara. It'd been a heady time for him...graduation from Pepperdine, work and practice at El Camino, then passing through the PGA regional Q-School qualification stages. Now, it was on to Q-School with Matt as his caddie.

"I feel like I'm ready for the final test. Did okay in the regionals." Scott took a sip of Coors. "Hope I didn't screw up your tour schedule."

"No way. I've been on the bag for the same guy for three years, ever since the Nationwide Tour, and after he passed at Q-School making it to the PGA."

"I followed your player on the sport page each Monday. He made a lot of money." Scott looked from Matt's patio at the pool and view from his condo. "Looks like your share was enough to buy these digs and more."

"Yeah, we did well. My player was a little pissed when I told him I was leaving, but he understood more when I explained that you and I'd planned this since we were kids."

"Could you get back with him if I don't make it?"

"That's what he promised, but you're going to make it...then the El Camino team will start its domination of the tour." Matt punched his fist on Scott's and a wide grin showed a row of straight white teeth in a smile no longer inhibited by the braces of his teenage years. His long auburn hair was gathered in a ponytail. And Matt was the model of a California surfer, lean and brown. His zest for rap music now swung toward jazz.

"Hey, Matt, what's with that little gold earring hanging on your left lobe?"

"Thought you'd never ask. It's just a token of self-expression for this golf bag toting Sherpa. Matt flicked his ear lobe with an index finger. His face turned serious when he asked, "how's your mother, the queen of mean, doing?" He thought that question sounded too harsh. "Sorry, Scott, I shouldn't have said that."

"That's okay, it fits. She's busy getting richer. We don't communicate much...never watched me play a golf match at Pepperdine. I moved to an apartment in El Cajon after college. She divorced that tennis pro who called golf, *pasture pool*. But the good news is she's seeing a shrink on a weekly basis."

"Good, maybe she'll sort out her feelings about golf and other stuff. How did you make it four years at Pepperdine without any dough from her?"

"Golf scholarship and working summers for Sandy got me through by the skin of my teeth."

Matt's expression showed concern for his friend's lack of support from his mother. "Would you believe my mom married a marine major after all that anti-war stuff she was into?"

"Things have a way of changing after five years, Matt. How did it go when you looped for that lady on the European tour?"

"That's a long story, but the bottom line is, she's a possessive bitch and I ended up getting fired by her."

Matt obviously didn't want to expand on the firing incident, so Scott didn't question him further.

***

Later, while Matt was busy grilling steaks, Scott moved over to the railing on the flagstone patio. He looked out at the stream of lights meandering down the hillside until they reached the pool of yellow that was the city of Santa Barbara, and he remembered a story Sandy McNair had told him about an incident during the Second World War near what's now the Sandpiper Golf Course.

"Matt, where's the Sandpiper course?"

Matt left the barbecue grill and ambled over to the railing beside Scott. He pointed to the western shoreline. "It's in Goleta, right about there."

"Did you know that back in the early forties a Japanese submarine lobbed a couple of shells into a refinery next to the course?"

"No, that's news. Who told you?"

"Sandy did."

"I guess Sandy filled you in on a lot of things besides golf stuff, Scott."

Scott thought about how Sandy would sprinkle history and even mathematics into golf talk and lessons. "Yeah, he'd teach me the history and geographical features about an interesting thing near where he'd visited a golf course. When he talked about course ratings and slopes he'd give me examples of the math to determine them. Then he'd make me work out a few hypothetical ratings."

"That's probably why you made scholar/athlete status at Pepperdine."

"How did you know about that?"

"When I worked the tournament at Torrey Pines in the San Diego area I visited Sandy, Hard Ass Harry Gladstone and Billy McGinnis. Sandy told me how well you were doing at Pepperdine. You're his pride and joy, dude."

"We've both come a long way up from when we started with Sandy and Hard Ass. Harry and Billy really helped you turn it around."

"I did show some attitude then, but..." Matt pointed to his cap that had the visor in the front and they both laughed. "Yeah, even though I didn't do the college bit like you, Sandy shared some things about caddying on tour passed on to him by those PGA players whose golf swings he tweaked. Both Harry and Billy were tough but effective, and they'll be my friends for life."

Scott looked back down the slope, past the shoreline and out to the lights on the oil rigs beyond. "Sandy is as good as any father could ever have been to me."

"Maybe a grandfather...whatever. Have you told Sandy that?"

"No, but I will next time I see him."

***

In the morning they drove along Big Sur toward the Monterey Peninsula, host for Q-School at its Poppy Hills and Spyglass Hill courses. The blue Pacific was breaking on white beach sand to their left and the Santa Lucia Mountains rose gently on the right to form a corridor of beauty. Waves crashed on the rocks below, and a white speckle of seabirds darted between the blue ocean and sky. They enjoyed the scenery but they chatted endlessly about golf.

Scott started picking Matt's brain about the tour: "What's this stuff I hear about guys playing in the zone? I've probably been there when I'm playing great but don't recognize the feeling. The television commentators make it sound like some kind of mystical state."

"It's media hype. Like in any sport...it's keeping your head in the game and your ass behind you. In other words...maintaining focus and alignment just like Sandy told us."

"Yeah, he made it sound less mysterious."

Scott took his eyes off the road for a moment and looked over at Matt. "I don't have a lot of bucks to survive on tour unless I make some cuts."

"Let's not think about cuts right now. Let's concentrate on Monterey and Q-School."

"Okay, but what's the real cost of us staying there? I've heard a lot of numbers."

Matt paused for a moment before answering. "Between twenty-five hundred and three-thousand a week for travel, motels, entry fees, food and incidentals. Plus, you're going to need to buy a different outfit for every day of play, including sweaters and rain gear. A clothing company won't endorse you until you're among the top fifty players or so."

"More bucks than I thought. Lot of motivation to make cuts and be around on Saturday."

"Any sponsors?" Matt asked.

"Only one. Some of the members at El Camino volunteered, but I didn't want any one else."

"Who've you got?"

"Sandy," Scott answered.

"Old Sandy McNair has the bucks. I'll never forget him paying for my braces." Matt beamed his perfect smile at Scott. "See?"

Scott laughed. "Can't call you Bucky Pearl anymore," Scott said. "By the way, Sandy is almost broke. He lost heavy on some bad investments. Even so, he insisted on giving me the regional entry fees so I could get to Q-School."

"Didn't know that about Sandy. How about you getting a loan from your mom?"

"Forget it. We hardly speak and there's no way she'll subsidize my golf 'fling,' as she calls it."

Matt looked over at him with concern. "Okay, let's do Q-School and face the money problem when and if we have to."

7

Q-School was the yearly examination prescribed by golf officialdom, the Professional Golfers Association (PGA), to graduate deserving new members into the highest competitive level of golf, the PGA Tour. It also gave those tour members who'd flunked the criterion to stay on tour a chance to get back. The initial Q-School agenda included classroom participation. It was later canceled by popular demand, but the "school" title remained.

After two practice rounds, the real part of "Hell Week" started for Scott at Spyglass Hill. It was the first of six days in the tension-packed golf crucible where one errant approach shot or one piddling-pulled 2-foot putt could cause failure to qualify. It was a grueling six rounds, consisting of 108 holes that were a test of golf skills like no other, and the odds for survival were not favorable. Just 140 players from the thousands worldwide had passed the regionals and made it on to Q-School. And only those players who scored within the top 30, including those that tied that number, would qualify to join the PGA Tour. The others would receive the 'minor league' Nationwide Tour status or a conditional status on the same tour.

***

On the practice range, Scott started working up through all thirteen clubs in his bag, beginning with the wedge. Matt handed him his lob wedge. "This one was paid for by Sandy?"

Scott laughed and said, "It's the legal one."

Scott stroked a few putts on the practice green until he was called to the tee. He shook hands with the official starter and was introduced to the other players of his threesome. One member of his group was a returning PGA Tour veteran. Bob Bray's game had degraded beyond 125th on the tour's list of money earned. He'd lost his PGA card, or his license to play a tournament without getting an exemption from a tournament sponsor. Matt knew Bray and set up a practice round between him and Scott. During the match Bob shared a few tips on tour play with Scott.

Scott was nervous during the introductions. Last-minute whispers transpired between he and Matt. The thought of being on the first tee, starting the first round of golf to begin what's known by the players as "Hell Week" was getting to him. Scott felt the nerve filaments making his arms and legs shake, and the butterflies buzzing around in his stomach seemed large as hummingbirds.

The first at Spyglass was a 595-yard-par-5 hole. A 14-mph wind was in the players' faces, and none would try reaching the green in two. Bray was first to tee off. The five-foot-eight Tom Watson lookalike completed his pre-shot routine, stepped up to his address position and hit a drive 278 yards down the middle of the fairway. Bray caught Scott's eye with a wink, and a smile of relief as he picked up his tee. His facial cast seemed to carry the hope this first shot was an omen to follow him in the week ahead...a chance to regain his livelihood.

It was Scott's turn. Those in the gallery watched as the PGA Tour candidate took his driver from Matt and placed his ball on the tee. They saw a handsome six-foot-three golfer with most of his long blond hair gathered by a visor, and the rest left free to move in the wind. His shoulders were broad, stomach flat and hips narrow. When Scott was introduced he sent a smile toward the crowd's polite applause. Then his face changed to a grim expression of serious purpose as his eyes focused on a spot far out on the fairway. His pre-shot routine brought him behind the ball with the driver in his right hand. He set-up in his stance. When he looked down at the ball his nervousness of before subsided. He gripped the club with his left hand turned inward so he could see three knuckles there and wiggled the driver a few times. His eyes narrowed in on a tree in the distance standing straight and tall, well beyond his intended target. Matt's yardage book dictated that the ball must carry 270 yards and catch a down slope to the left before rolling 15 yards to an ideal position for the second shot.

Scott placed his driver head behind the ball, took a deep breath, and made his back swing. At the top of it, his club hesitated for a second. The driver started down in a smooth accelerating motion that peaked to a speed of 118 miles per hour when it made contact with the ball. His swing was still in the process of follow-through when he heard the *oohs* and *ahs* of the gallery followed by their applause. The ball landed 20 yards beyond the place Matt had designated.

A three-iron and the *legal* lob wedge got him on the green where he sunk a six-footer for a birdie to start "Hell Week." Scott played the first five holes of the Spyglass course at three under par and finished the first day two under. After checking the leader board he knew he was still in the hunt.

***

Scott's next four rounds went well enough to place him within the players that were still in contention for a tour card. But on the sixth and last round he encountered bad weather at Poppy Hills. The Monterey Peninsula was hit by a storm that came in from the Pacific to buffet the Linksland. It brought with it a deluge of horizontal rain driven by gusts as strong as thirty miles per hour. It was rare weather for a San Diego native to experience, but not enough cause, without accompanying thunder and lightning, for the officials to suspend play.

The storm could've washed Scott out of Q-School if not for Matt's experience with these same conditions when at British Open venues in England and Scotland. Matt had checked the forecast earlier and made his golf bag ready for it. Out on the course he continually wiped down the grips, handing Scott a dry glove on every other tee and kept an umbrella over his player between shots and putts. Scott finished with a 76.

They walked toward the locker room "What do you think about our chances, Matt?"

"Well, no one has made par for the round yet." Just then a gust of wind blew away a towel draped over his shoulder. After chasing it, Matt said, "the wind is getting worse. The guys out there now are going to play hell staying out of the 80s."

They left the cold, rain-swept course and drove back to town not knowing if today's 76, placing Scott's total for Q-School at five under par for the six rounds, would be enough to qualify.

***

Exhausted and chilled from over five hours of wet, battering gusts, they sought the warm welcome of the motel Jacuzzi. It would be another hour before all the players finished, and they'd know if their score was good enough to earn the right to play on the PGA Tour. They tried to relax in the soothing whirl despite growing more eager by the minute to know their fate.

After they left the Jacuzzi, showered and dressed, Matt fiddled nervously with his gold earring while he called the Poppy Hills locker room attendant on his cell phone. Claudio Spencer, Bob Bray's caddie, had just finished and the attendant put him on.

"Hey, Claudio, how was it?"

"Hell, I haven't been blown around like this since Scotland, Matt. Everyone's finished and my bag shot a seventy-eight."

"Did Bob Bray make it, Claudio?"

"Yeah, he squeaked into last place, tied at four under par for the six rounds."

Matt yelled, even though Scott's ear was only six inches from the cell phone, "Scott, we're in! Our five under made it! The El Camino kids will do the tour together."

Scott's grin was wide and, after a few seconds, he asked, "When, and where do we start?"

"It won't begin for us until Hawaii at Kapalua, the second week of January."

"Not a bad place to begin for a surfing caddie, Matt."

"You'll need some clothes, Scott. You can't wear chinos and those faded old shirts on tour. Like I told you, it's a different outfit for every day out there."

Scott frowned. "I didn't figure on clothing expenses."

"I've got a friend in Carmel who owns a clothing store, and he'll give me credit until we make a check," Matt offered. "You're about the same build as Ernie Els and not in to the tight-fitting Adam Scott stuff. So we'll go with the clothing line Els wears."

"I'm thinking I'll dress more like Duffy Waldorf, with tie-dyed shirts and pants."

"You've gotta be kidding, Scott."

***

Scott picked out eight shirts, eight pairs of slacks to match, and four sweaters at Farley's on Main Street in Monterey. After they finished shopping, it was time to celebrate.

They began with a steak cooked over mesquite wood accompanied by a Napa Valley merlot. After the meal they roamed the music bars until settling in one. A jazz group's mellow saxophones and muted trumpets were playing their arrangement of "Night Train" when two attractive women walked by and sat down at a table next to theirs.

Matt leaned toward Scott. "I'm going to ask them to join us."

Scott nodded slowly. "Okay, ask them."

Both were law students from New York City in Monterey on vacation. It was a good departure from a week of intense golf to hear their slant on other things about New York City and the law.

They left the Jazz Lounge and found a place on the waterfront with live dance music. Scott was enjoying the company of Lizbeth Sweeney. She told him about her large Irish family and injected her sense of humor in the right places. At around midnight Lizbeth told him she had to leave, and explained why. She had to rise at five in the morning to make her flight to New York. Scott thought it best he got some sleep, so he offered to walk her to her hotel. Matt and his new friend stayed to dance the night away.

About halfway to Lizbeth's hotel, the storm that'd plagued the Monterey Peninsula all day gave a parting blast in the form of a deluge. They ran the rest of the way but arrived in the hotel lobby dripping wet.

"Scott, look at you," she said. "You're soaked. Come, I have plenty of dry towels in my room."

Later, Lizbeth came out of the bathroom wrapped in a white terrycloth robe, courtesy of the hotel. She was carrying an armful of fluffy white towels. Scott wiped most of the wet from his clothes and hair. A dry towel was left over.

"Your hair's still wet...here, let me," he said.

Scott took the towel and started rubbing her head, noting that the raven mass of hair was even curlier wet than dry, and the color went well with an attractive face that was not impaired by a tiny cluster of freckles on each side of a slightly upturned nose.

After a vigorous rub he said, "there, that's got it."

Lizbeth looked up at him from her barefoot five-foot-seven height before their kiss. She had the largest brown eyes Scott has ever seen. His arms encircled her, and he could feel her firm body pressing hard against his own.

***

It was two in the morning when Scott returned to the motel. Matt was asleep in the other twin. He took a small piece of paper with Lizbeth's phone number on it out of his pocket and placed it on the nightstand with his wallet and watch. When he did that, he noticed the red message light on the phone flashing. He called the front desk. One call was from the assistant pro at El Camino, Al Ingalls. Scott thought Al just wanted to congratulate him...too late to call him back. He'd phone Al in the morning.

***

The phone call to Al Ingalls at eight in the morning brought sad news.

"Sandy dead?"

"Yeah, Scott. He passed away last evening, sometime around six, after he got a call from the head- pro at Poppy Hills telling him you'd made it."

Scott's thoughts began in a spiral. *Sandy was ninety-three and sick, but still...*"What about arrangements?"

"None." Al said. "You know, he doesn't have any relatives. It'll probably be a quick burial."

"No way, Al. You know he saved me from trouble and helped to get me here. He got Matt on tour as a caddie and has helped many others, like you. We need to celebrate Sandy's life."

"I'll be in San Diego to make the arrangements this afternoon. Book the function room at El Camino for Monday evening." Scott paused. He recalled Sandy's love for bagpipe music. "I'll call the Clan Campbell bagpipers to play and contact the newspaper to announce the celebration at El Camino in Sandy's obituary."

"Who's gonna pay for all this, Scott? Sandy was broke."

"I am. I just won twenty-five large at Q-School, and Sandy had a lot to do with it."

"Okay, Scott, and by the way, congratulations."

SAN DIEGO

8

More than 300 came to El Camino Country Club for the celebration of Sandy's life. Many who'd benefited from his instruction were there, including some who'd gone on to the Champions, PGA, Nationwide and LPGA tours. On Tuesday morning, The Clan Campbell bagpipers dressed in their plaid kilts led a procession to the practice range where Sandy's ashes were lowered in a grave marked by a simple epigraph etched on a small marble stone:

SANDY MCNAIR 1920—2013
HE CAME FROM ST. ANDREWS
TO TEACH THE GAME OF GOLF

"Could you come to my office tomorrow at nine?"

It was Frank Dyer, an El Camino member and local attorney, who caught up to Scott as he walked slowly from the grave-site blinking back tears. He stopped walking. "What's up, Frank?"

"I'm executor of Sandy's estate, and he left everything to you."

Scott glanced back at the marble stone for a moment without responding to Dyer.

The lawyer broke into Scott's silence. "Sandy didn't leave much behind. He was generous to a fault and got taken in by a crooked investment counselor. But there are some books and old golf things he brought with him when he left Saint Andrews. They're all yours."

***

Scott was at the law office the next day with Matt. Attorney Dyer filled his conference table with all of Sandy's worldly possessions. There were a few antique golf clubs, oil paintings of St. Andrews, old golf books and a bronze, *Oscar*-sized statuette of a nude woman swinging a golf club. A journal compiled by Hugh McNair was also in the mix. It included newspaper articles dated from the nineteenth century telling of Hugh's various feats in golf and feathery ball making business at St. Andrews. The author of one article had spent a day with Hugh during his record round.

Scott signed some papers the lawyer put before him. Afterwards, with Matt's help, he started packing the items he had inherited in a carton supplied by Dyer. Scott hesitated before placing a five by five-inch wooden box in with the other things. He was curious about it, and studied the box for a moment before sliding the cover back along some grooves to expose the contents.

Matt looked over Scott's shoulder and down into the box. He said, "hey, you've got yourself an old feathery golf ball."

Scott stared down at the almost round tan object and saw the name **HUGH** and the numbers 26 and 78 inscribed in black ink on the leather. Inside the box, next to the feathery, were two slips of paper. One was a note to Scott from Sandy and the other, on stiffer stock, yellowed with age, was Hugh McNair's record score card with a few words written at the bottom.

The note from Sandy:

Dear Scott,
I wanted you to have this feathery used by my great-grandfather,
Hugh McNair, when he set a record at the old course at St. Andrews
in 1849.

Sandy.

The aged parchment contained the hole-by-hole scores of Hugh McNair's record round. The note scribbled at the bottom read:

Played a match with Willie Dunn of Musselburgh, backed by Mr.
Brown of Balgarvie, winning it, and scored a record 78. My 26
pennyweight feathery ball worked well in the calm air.

The scorecard was signed and dated July 8, 1849 by Hugh McNair, and attested by The Society of St. Andrews Golfers.

Matt examined the scorecard and the note from Sandy. "You might be able to sell this feathery golf ball for a good price."

Scott slowly slid the cover back on the box. "I'd like to keep it. I think it's what Sandy would want me to do."

Matt gave him a look of concern and said, "hope that works out for you."

9

While still in the San Diego area before starting out on tour, Scott wanted to evaluate his present set of golf clubs and make any necessary changes. Sandy had bought him a set from Linksking Golf before he entered Pepperdine, and at that time he'd introduced him to Mark Breen, CEO of that club-making company. Mark attended the celebration of Sandy's life at El Camino, and Scott set up an appointment with Mark to have a Linksking technician make sure his clubs still matched his swing.

Scott met Linksking's club-fitting expert, Charlie Davis. Charlie was a thin man in his fifties with John Lennon-type glasses whose hands stayed put in his leather apron pockets until they were needed. Charlie recorded Scott's physical measurements and swing characteristics on the range. If necessary, a set of new customized Linksking clubs would be made from these data.

A golf swing analyzer called the *Swing Groover* was part of the test equipment used at the range. Scott swung a driver and a five iron as the *Swing Groover* monitored his swing path, swing speed, golf ball launch speed and ball spin revolutions per minute. (SRPM). These data would be used to select a shaft with the right kick point and flex. The contact of the golf ball at impact, relative to the perfect sweet spot, was recorded by Charlie with impact tape to determine the best loft and lie angles for Scott's irons.

Through this testing, Charlie determined that Scott's swing parameters would be better served with a new set of clubs. His present set didn't perfectly match his golf swing according to the *Swing Groover* print-out, and Scott agreed, knowing a player on tour must strive for equipment perfection. He ordered a new set built to the test specifications measured by Charlie and his machine. He kept only two clubs from his old set—his putter and the 60-degree lob wedge Sandy had given him.

He picked up his new set of clubs from Charlie two days later. They worked out fine on the range. He attempted to pay for them, but

Mark Breen had left directions with Charlie that the clubs were to be complimentary.

***

Scott entered Mark's office. "Hey, Mark, thanks for the donation."

"No problem. I'd do anything to help one of Sandy's kids." He got up from his desk to shake Scott's hand. "Good luck on tour. If you score well using our clubs and like them, we'll hire you to endorse them."

Scott left Linksking and went out to Torrey Pines to play a round of golf with his new clubs on the North Course there. The clubs passed his on-course trial, and he was ready to test them in the real world of golf...at the PGA Tour in Kapalua, Hawaii.

NEW YORK

10

Scott missed the cut at Kapalua by two strokes. Then he missed five more cuts after that. Finally, the Buick Invitational at Torrey Pines, a familiar track, earned him a check for $8,225. Out of the next twelve tournaments his earnings totaled only $22,000, and there wasn't any other income coming in from golf product endorsements for the fledgling Q-School qualifier.

Scott had just missed a cut at Westchester Country Club in New York, and it was another Friday evening of disappointment. He was with Matt in their motel room trying to figure out what had gone wrong with his game.

"The competition out here is more than I thought. I've been missing cuts by only a few strokes. What can I do, Matt?"

"Make more putts."

"Sure, just like that."

Matt took the putter out of Scott's golf bag and ran his hand down the shaft to the head, then took a sheet of paper from his wallet that had Scott's playing statistics on it. He scanned down the playing categories before fixing his eyes on three of them.

"You're on most greens in regulation or better, but weak in birdies and eagles after you get there. The clubs you got from Linksking are working out fine. It's your putting that's doing you in. That old caddie saying holds true: 'A player *w*ho putts for pars is like a dog that chases cars...he doesn't survive.' You need to drop more putts in for birdies and even a few eagles."

Scott took his putter from Matt and started making short strokes at an imaginary ball. "It's the same putting stroke and putter I've used since Pepperdine. It got me through Q-School."

"I know, but I've seen a change in putters make good things happen." Matt's eyes narrowed and he looked straight at Scott. "A player's confidence will improve after that." Matt took the putter from Scott and put it back in the golf bag. He picked up a box with a dozen golf balls in it. "Let's go, there's a course with a practice green near here."

***

They selected five putters from a rack in the pro shop. The putter heads were of different configurations. They had shafts of varying lengths and off-sets. Matt stationed himself near a cup on the putting green and rolled the balls back while Scott stroked putts from fifteen feet with each of the putters. His stroke with one of the putters was rolling the golf ball in the cup consistently.

They bought the putter, and stayed on the practice green for two hours trying putts from various distances and contours. Most dropped in the cup, and Scott's confidence started back up the road to restoration.

***

Back at the motel, they ordered submarine sandwiches and tackled another problem.

Scott was putting into a drinking glass set down on the carpet ten feet away with his new putter when he said, "I'm almost broke. Just enough to get us to San Diego and regroup. I can't make expenses for the next tour stop."

"Whoa." Matt took a bite from his sub and chewed it slowly while he mind-counted his assets. "I've got enough dough to get us through the tournament at the TPC in Maryland week after next and a little more if we need it. We're off next week, anyway, since we're out of the US Open."

Scott sat down on the bed and reached for his sandwich. "Thanks. I'll pay you back with interest soon as I can. Any suggestions on where we go next week before Maryland?"

Matt took a long swig from a Pepsi can. "Bray and his caddie, Claudio Spencer, are out of the Open because Bray's wife is due to have a baby and he wants to be with her. Claudio invited me to stay at his place on Long Island, and it has room for you. You can practice at a course nearby."

"That'll work. I've got to win something in Maryland."

When Scott said that, Matt noticed the expression on his friend's face. It showed his desperation over finances.

Matt stood up to face Scott sitting on his bed. "You can't stay under the financial gun any longer, like needing to make a check in Maryland to stay on tour. The pressure of earning enough for our expenses is screwing up your concentration. You need a good checking account balance to ease that worry."

"How do I get that kind of dough?"

Matt gave his friend a hard look. "If you don't want any sponsors, you've got to sell the golf antiques Sandy left you."

Scott was quiet for a few seconds before slowly nodding his head in reluctant agreement.

***

The next day they were on Long Island, New York, when Matt asked Claudio Spencer, "Do you know anyone around here who can tell us about selling golf antiques?"

They'd just finished playing a round at a course on Long Island, and Matt and Claudio were having a beer in the clubhouse. Scott went straight to the practice green from the course even though he'd made seven birdies and shot a 66 using his new putter.

Matt looked across the table at Claudio while waiting for an answer. He saw his friend with swarthy skin and large dark eyes run his fingers through his curly jet-black hair as he thought about someone to help with the antique golf stuff. Finally, he touched his Roman nose with an index finger and his face brightened with an idea.

"Yeah, my Uncle Anthony has all kinds of connections in the New York area."

"In golf antiques, Claudio?"

"In all things. He's my mother's brother, and they came here from Sicily before I was born. I'll give him a call." Claudio reached for his cell phone and touched some numbers, hesitating before entering the last one. "Where are these antiques?"

"On the way to your apartment from San Diego by UPS. They'll be here tomorrow morning."

Claudio greeted his uncle and made small phone talk before mentioning the antiques.

"Matt, my uncle wants a friend to see them."

Matt thought it would be okay with Scott and said, "sure, when?"

Claudio asked his uncle. "He said tomorrow evening at seven...my place."

11

T wo men accompanied Anthony Imperato to Claudio's apartment. One was dressed like Claudio's uncle in an Armani suit with a black silk shirt and a wide-white necktie of the same material. Uncle Anthony's friend's wavy white hair was a vivid contrast to the dark skin of his face. He was introduced as Mario Carrabba, a collector of golf antiques and memorabilia.

The other man was large, over six feet and stocky. He wore a black leather jacket over a turtleneck shirt of the same color. The turtleneck didn't hide the thick gold chain looped around his neck. His head was shaved of all hair and so shiny it mirrored the kitchen lighting. Carrabba introduced him as his chauffeur, Rocco, but he looked and acted more like the stereotypical bodyguard.

The golf antiques were spread out on the kitchen table. Mario examined each item in detail. He held the nude bronze statuette of the naked woman golfer in his hand and said, "bella! bella!" His companions laughed.

Rocco repeated Mario's remark with his own interpretation in crude English. "Good-looking broad."

Mario briefly scrutinized the books and old golf clubs before he slid open the cover of the box with the feathery golf ball inside. Carrabba stared at the feathery for a few minutes before taking some white silk gloves from the inside pocket of his suit coat and slipping them on. He addressed those watching him with a New York City inflected Italian accent. "You must not touch this ball with bare hands or the oil of your skin will ruin the leather."

Mario took a jeweler's loupe from another pocket and picked up the feathery. He examined the numbers 26 and 78 inscribed on the leather with the name, **HUGH**, while holding the loupe up against one eye. When finished, he put the feathery back in the box. He studied Sandy's note and the yellowed parchment showing McNair's record score at St. Andrews in 1849.

Carrabba slowly placed the loupe and gloves back in the inside pocket of his suit coat and spoke to Scott, "I'd like to talk alone to my friends for a few moments."

Uncle Anthony and Mario's so-called chauffeur joined Carrabba in a room off the kitchen.

Anthony spoke first. "What's up, Mario?"

"Mama mia, Tony! This golfing guy, Beckman, doesn't have a clue of what he's got in that box."

"Is that the funny-looking ball you looked at for so long, Mario?" Anthony asked.

"Christ, yes. That feathery has been lost for years. Collectors all over the world have been looking for it. It's very valuable...almost priceless. I've gotta have it in my collection, Tony, before anyone else gets wind of the find."

"What's the problem, Mario? Just offer the guy a low-ball figure," Rocco injected. "He doesn't know shit from Shineola about how much it's worth, and he needs money. You can stiff him."

"Hey, wait a minute, you guys, my nephew is the one who turned you on to this, and he's straight. He's just trying to help a friend who needs money to stay on the golf tour."

Rocco spoke up again. "Bring the nephew in here and ask him how much this guy needs to play golf for a year on the tour if he doesn't win enough for expenses."

Claudio was summoned from the kitchen.

Claudio told them about tour expenses. "It takes at least a hundred grand a year to meet expenses for a player and his caddie." He looked at Mario Carrabba and said, "don't screw Scott, he's a friend."

Carrabba narrowed his eyes and stared at Claudio. The index finger of his right hand touched his thumb. He wriggled his wrist close to Claudio's face. "Hey, I'm talkin to you, kid...listen. This is my business. Let it alone. I'll make a deal the golfer can't refuse."

***

After they returned to the kitchen, Carrabba sent Rocco to the car for the cash. He came back with a black leather satchel and plunked it down on the table beside the golf antiques. Carrabba opened the bag and Scott, Matt and Claudio saw $100 bills wrapped with rubber bands stacked inside. Matt whistled.

Carrabba gave Scott a hard look. "There's one hundred grand cash in the bag. That's my offer."

Scott was in shock. He was surprised at the value and thrilled that the money would allow him to play worry-free on tour. But caution started to creep in.

Rocco pushed the satchel full of cash at Scott. "Take it, it's tax free."

The fast cash offer and pressure made Scott hesitate. He was becoming more suspicious as to the real value of the antiques."I need a day to think it over, Mr. Carrabba. He indicated the golf antiques spread out on the table. "I inherited them from a good friend, and I may want to keep some."

"You what?" Rocco came on strong. "Are you wasting our time?" He was now so close to Scott's face that the next words came with breath tainted with garlic. "If you're smart you'll make the deal with Mr. Carrabba right now and not fuck around with anyone else."

Rocco started to move in closer to Scott before his boss stopped him with an outstretched arm and said, "okay, Rock, that's enough. Sorry, Mr. Beckman, Rocco gets carried away when I don't get what I want. You need a day? That's okay. Call me tomorrow."

Carrabba handed Scott a card and headed for the door. Uncle Anthony kissed his nephew on both cheeks, and followed behind Carrabba. Rocco snatched the satchel from the table, scowled at Scott and left the apartment behind the others.

After a squeal of rubber accentuated an angry departure by Rocco at the wheel, Scott asked, "Hey, Claudio what's with those guys?"

"Like I told you, Uncle Anthony has all kinds of connections. Had no clue before this that one of his friends would play hardball to get some golf antiques."

"Matt, you're awful quiet. What's your take?"

"I think I just lived through a scene from *The Sopranos*. What now, Scott?"

"I'm going to call this antique dealer I know who's a member at El Camino. He doesn't do golf stuff, but maybe he can steer me in the right direction to get an honest appraisal around here."

After he finished the call, Scott told them the results. "He recommended an auction gallery in New York City. Claudio, can I borrow your car tomorrow?"

"Sure, only you'll have to clean out the trunk to fit in those antiques. It's filled with my PGA tour survival kit."

***

Later, Scott took a small piece of paper from his wallet. Written on it was Lizbeth Sweeney's phone number. He made the call and connected with the lady he had met in Monterey. They set a time and place to meet in New York City.

12

The Covington Gallery security guard was an older man in uniform. The plaque on his desk was engraved with the name, LEM SHATTUCK. He was pleasant, but with a policeman's authoritative manner. He stood up from his desk in the lobby to ask the nature of Scott's business. Satisfied, he phoned Jason Gamby, the golf antique and memorabilia specialist for the gallery. While waiting for Gamby, Shattuck chatted with them. It turned out he was an avid golfer and a fan of the PGA.

"When I retired from the NYPD, I was planning to move to Florida, play golf five days a week and watch all the PGA tournaments there," Shattuck said.

Matt asked the obvious question. "What changed your plan?"

"It turns out my honest cop retirement pension isn't enough to cover buying or renting a condo and paying greens fees. So I'll work here and save up enough to get down there eventually."

Scott said, "good luck in retirement Mr. Shattuck."

"And the same to you on tour, Scott." And he asked for Scott's autograph on a cap that already held those of Ernie Els and Tiger Woods. Scott was flattered to scrawl his name in their company.

Gamby entered the lobby. He was a tall thin man with sharp, angular features. A perfectly trimmed white goatee didn't match his long jet-black hair held back in a ponytail. Gamby looked over his small-rimmed glasses at Scott and Matt as if he was making a human appraisal before he would do the same with the golf antiques. His polite greeting came at them with a British accent.

Scott told Jason about Carrabba's offer, but Gamby didn't comment on the $100,000 amount. Instead he took a cart from a storage room behind the guard's desk. They helped him load the antiques onto it. Gamby left, wheeling the cart to a room where he and his staff would appraise the collection.

An hour later Gamby returned to the lobby. An expression of dismay was on his face and he shook his head. "Carrabba offered you one hundred thousand for the lot?"

"That's right. Do you know him?" Scott asked.

"The man is a scoundrel. He owns a golf course upstate, with a clubhouse full of museum-quality golf antiques to show off. I must say, some of the items were obtained by devious means." Gamby's eyes shifted between Scott and Matt before he continued in agitated words that didn't guard his native Yorkshire dialect. "Carrabba knows the worth of that feathery, and that bugger tried to steal the bloody ball from you."

"What's it worth?" Scott asked.

"The feathery alone at auction could be bid up at well over a million." Gamby rolled his eyes toward the ceiling. "Packaged with the score card signed by the Society of Saint Andrews Golfers, along with McNair's journal, further authenticating the record...who knows how much higher it could go?" Gamby continued in the same high-pitched voice caused by his excitement over the feathery. "The Royal and Ancient would have dearly wanted the feathery donated to a museum when found, but evidently Sandy McNair decided to keep it in his family before he left it to you. Collectors have been seeking this lost treasure for years."

Scott was stunned. After a few minutes, he recovered enough to ask Gamby. "How about the other things in the collection?"

"The old books, clubs and paintings should get bids totaling between one hundred and one-hundred, fifty thousand. The bronze statuette of the nude woman golfer is unique. That bronze came from the studio of Rodin in Paris around 1865, according to the mark on the base. The circumstances on how and why it got to Scotland and into Hugh McNair's possession require some research before an estimated value can be established."

"What happens now?"

"Well, if you'd like Covington Gallery to represent you at auction, we may proceed," Gamby said.

Scott glanced over at Matt and saw him shrug his shoulders. His palms-up gesture was like when the club selection for a golf shot was Scott's final call, not his. Scott reasoned for a time about his decision before answering Gamby. *Would Sandy want me to keep the feathery? But I need the money to continue playing, and I'm certain he'd want me to do that.*

Scott's sigh was edged in regret and some sadness. "Okay, let's do the auction."

They left the lobby for Gamby's office where he explained the auction process to Scott. "You must consign the collection to Covington Gallery. We will make up an announcement in brochure format that'll describe the items and include the time and place for previewing the auction. The announcement will be sent by email and target a select list of collectors whose interest we know to be high."

"Will the auction be here in New York?"

"No, Scott, we'll hold it in our London gallery. After I appraised the lot I phoned our owner to confirm the London location. She's very excited about the find. Sarah Covington played on the European Women's Tour for five years before she inherited the gallery from her mother. Sarah's an avid collector of golf antiques with early Saint Andrews origination."

The name, Covington as part of the Gallery, got Matt's attention when he first heard it, but he cast aside any connection with Sarah Covington other than a name coincidence until Gamby spoke about the owner. Matt thought, *Damn it, that's her! I'll warn Scott about Sarah when the time is right, but while doing the deal, he doesn't need that confusion.*

"Why is the auction in London, Mr. Gamby?" Scott asked.

"Keen interest in the collection centers in Great Britain, Ireland and, of course, Scotland. Collectors from the United States and other countries not in attendance will be connected by satellite link to our auction in London and bids may come in by phone."

"Covington's commission?" Scott asked.

"We contract for twenty percent of the collection's value as sold."

"When would the auction take place, Mr. Gamby?"

"I must do some more thinking before we set a date, but my guess is in about four weeks from now."

Scott looked over at Matt. "Uh- oh."

Matt hesitated to calculate their expenses to stay on tour for four weeks. "Hey, my meager savings can cover a loan...and, Scott, your credit rating has just jumped to triple A."

Before Scott signed the contract with Covington, he removed Hugh McNair's journal from the collection, wanting to learn more about his mentor's famous relative and the feathery ball he had used when he set a record.

Gamby voiced his concerns about the journal leaving the collection. "As I said before, McNair's journal is a very valuable item when packaged with the feathery. Please take very good care of it. It would be best to wear these when you read it." He handed Scott a pair of latex gloves.

They took a last look at the feathery and the other antiques before all were locked in the Covington Gallery vault.

***

On the way out to Long Island, Matt told Scott about Sarah Covington. "Remember when we met at my place in Santa Barbara and you asked about my Europe gig?"

"Yeah, and you said you were fired by a player, and it was a long story."

"Well, the player was Sarah Covington, owner of Covington Gallery."

"Wow, it's a small golf-world. Why did she fire you, Matt? Did you club her wrong or something like that?"

"Not about my looping abilities. She did it because I had a relationship with another player she wanted to hit on, and I was in her way."

"Do you think I should continue to deal with Covington Gallery?"

"Probably be okay, Scott, but be careful. She's very possessive, and will do most anything to get what she wants."

13

When Scott finished reading the article by Alistair Beddington in Hugh McNair's journal written in 1849, he sat up on the couch and exclaimed, "Awesome!"

Matt looked up from the cribbage game. "What's awesome?"

Scott stood and shook the journal in Matt's direction. "I've just read how my feathery ball was made and then played in the match that set a record at Saint Andrews back in 1849."

Matt was curious. He put his cards down on the table. "Hey, let me read that."

"You should...McNair's caddie, James McEwan, was a red head like you and just as out of control. He handed the journal to Matt. "Be careful with it. I've got to return it to the gallery. You heard Gamby tell us how valuable it was."

Matt put the white-latex gloves on. "Okay," he said, "no beer stains."

***

In the early morning Scott, Matt and Claudio left for a nearby golf course and played 36 holes there. When they finished they went to the practice green and stroked putts for quarters. Scott won most of the money before they left to have lunch at the clubhouse restaurant. Scott told Claudio about the Covington Gallery appraisal for the golf antiques.

"Wow! I'm sorry I introduced you guys to that bastard Carrabba through my uncle. Glad you know the real value of the antiques now." He raised his glass of beer in a toast and took a sip. "It might be best, Scott, if you call Mario Carrabba to let him know his offer is rejected instead of leaving him hanging."

"Even though he tried to screw me?"

"Yeah, it's more of a sign of respect and a courtesy to my uncle and Carrabba. Kinda important in their circle."

"Okay, I'll do it." Scott reached in his wallet for Carrabba's card and made the call.

The voice that answered sounded like Rocco. "Who's this?"

Scott told him.

"It's you, the golfer? Mr. Carrabba was very disappointed when you didn't take his offer last night. And when Mr. Carrabba is disappointed, I get disturbed. You know what I'm sayin, golfer?"

The next voice on the phone was Carrabba's. "Hello, Mr. Beckman. I hope you've changed your mind."

"No, I haven't. I got a second opinion, and the golf antiques are worth much more than what you offered."

There was a ten-second pause before Carrabba responded. "Who?"

"Covington Gallery."

"That prick, Jason Gamby?"

"Right."

"I'll beat whatever that fag's gonna give you. I want that feathery."

"Too late, I've signed a contract with Covington to auction the collection."

There was some heavy breathing, and Scott heard what he guessed was a swear word in Italian. The phone connection was abruptly terminated.

Scott looked across the table at Matt and Claudio. "Mr. Carrabba was not pleased."

Matt placed his beer on the table. "If Carrabba wants the feathery so bad," he said, "he can bid on it at the auction."

"Make an honest man out of him, Matt. I'm ready to put Carrabba and the antique golf issues aside and head for Maryland tomorrow to take on the modern game. "But before then, I've got a date tonight in New York City with a lovely lady named Lizbeth."

"That the same brown-eyed gal with the curly black hair you met in Monterey?" Matt asked.

"You got it."

14

Scott drove from Claudio's apartment in Hempstead, Long Island, along route 495. He entered the city and arrived at the Covington Gallery just before five in the evening. The guard, Lem Shattuck, was at his desk in the lobby. In a hurry to meet Lizbeth, Scott gave the McNair journal to Lem to pass on to Gamby for shipment to London with the other antiques.

Lem reached for Scott's hand. "I'll catch you on the tour in Florida. I just gave my notice to quit. I retire at the end of the month and I've made a down payment on a condo in Ft. Meyers."

"Great, I'll look forward to seeing you there, Lem."

Scott left the Gallery on Madison Avenue and found a place to park near the theater district not too far from Sardis. He entered the restaurant and was led to a table where he waited for the arrival of Lizbeth Sweeney. She'd made the dinner reservation and had two tickets for a play. Scott was admiring the many caricature drawings of celebrities hung on the walls of Sardis when Lizbeth entered the restaurant and walked toward the table.

She was wearing a gray suit and carried a matching gray leather briefcase. Her hairstyle had changed since they had first met. The full, black, naturally-curly mass was now a shorter version than he'd rubbed dry in Monterey. Scott thought the hair style change gave her a professional lawyer look.

Scott stood up from the table and was deciding whether to hug her or not when Lizbeth made the decision for him. When she reached the table, her arms went around him. They stood looking at each other for a long time without speaking. The tiny freckles sprinkled beside her nose were still there and were perhaps made more vivid by some time in the sun. Her gaze continued to lock him in. He'd never seen eyes as expressive as hers, and the look in them turned to an inquisitive one when she sat down at the table.

"I've been following your tournament results in the paper every Monday morning. Is Matt Kemp still toting your bag?" She asked.

"Yeah, Matt's still puts up with me. I'm disappointed in my play, but I think it's going to turn around for the better soon."

"Why?"

"Got me a new putter."

"Really...sounds too simple."

"I know, but it seems to be working in practice. I'm going to test it this week in Maryland." Scott reached for her hand and looked deep into those incredible eyes. "How about you? How's the law business, Lizbeth?"

"Do me a favor." She smiled. "From now on call me Beth. No one could ever handle Lizbeth. They always want to turn Lizbeth into *Elizabeth*. Anyway, I'm out of law school...working for a firm in Manhattan and waiting to take the bar exam. I'll specialize in international law."

"Good for you, Liz."

They were laughing when the waiter came to take their order.

They ordered the special Sardis steak with *pomme frites* and shared a bottle of red wine from the Monterey as a nostalgic tribute to their meeting on that California peninsula. Conversation came easily...the meal was just right.

***

Scott's intention was to return to Long Island after the play because he would leave for Maryland early in the morning and wanted to be rested for the week ahead at the Booz Allen Tournament. But a lovely lady with large brown eyes tampered with those good intentions.

He arrived at Claudio's apartment a little after three in the morning. And they left for Maryland at eight, where he'd find out in the real world of tournament play if his new putter was the answer to his past putting woes.

CHICAGO

15

Scott finished, tied for fifth place at the Booz Allen Classic in Potomac, Maryland, and a check for $59,200 was deposited in his account. Then he received another check at the John Deere in Illinois for $36,600. His confidence soared the next week at the BMW Open outside of Chicago where he collected his fourth-place winnings of $181,800. The BMW finish qualified him to play at the British Open in July at Turnberry, Scotland.

"Over a quarter of a million, Scott, and a big-time golf club endorsement contract ready to sign with Linksking. Not too shabby. And just three weeks ago you were broke and missing putts and cuts. Money comes fast when you play well out here."

They were winding down from the excitement of being only five strokes away from winning it all at the BMW when the phone rang in their hotel room. It was Jason Gamby.

"First off, Scott, congratulations on a fine tournament. I watched all of it on television," Jason said.

"Thanks, Jason. What's going on with the auction?"

"Well, I have two pieces of good news. The announcements have been sent and the auction date is set for Wednesday-week. The response has been exceptional, based on excitement over the feathery."

"Sounds good. What else have you got?"

"I completed my research on the bronze female-golfer- statuette."

"And?"

"I found out a quite famous Parisian artist, Jacques Ramon, sculpted it in 1865. He studied under Rodin."

"Was golf popular in France then, Jason?" Scott asked.

"Not really...until 1907 when a Frenchman won the Open. Anyway, during a trip to Scotland, Ramon became intrigued with the game and met Hugh McNair at Saint Andrews. When he returned to the studio, Ramon sculpted the work with one of Rodin's ballerina models posing nude as the golfer."

Scott recalled the graceful pose of the statuette, and it was like a ballerina's. "How many others were made, Jason.?"

"That's the best part. My research shows that Master Rodin was not pleased with the work. He thought the sculptor's effort was frivolous and of no commercial value, so he ordered the mold destroyed. It's one of a kind and the first known bronze of a woman golfer."

"How did it get to Sandy?" Scott asked.

"Ramon made another journey to Saint Andrews and presented his work to McNair at a ceremony presided over and recorded by what was then called The Society of Saint Andrews Golfers...now, The Royal and Ancient Golf Society of Saint Andrews. Hugh must have passed it on to someone in his family, and the statuette ended up with your friend Sandy."

"What's it worth, Jason?"

"It should fetch over $500,000 at auction."

A new plan started to race around in Scott's head.

He had about $150,000 in his bank account after paying off what he owed Matt. The statuette would bring $500,000 more. The books and clubs were worth another $150,000. He was playing well and was looking forward to more winnings. There was also a lucrative golf product endorsement contract for him in final negotiation with Linksking Golf.

"I say, Scott, are you still there?"

Gamby's voice brought him out of his reverie. "Yeah...uh...Jason, I've just decided to keep the feathery."

It was Gamby's turn to pause. He let Scott's revelation sink in... "You can't...you have a contract with Covington. The announcements are out, and the feathery is the principal attraction of the auction."

"I want it back, Mr. Gamby."

"Scott, there'll be a large penalty invoked if you remove the feathery from our auction."

"How much?"

"The contract states that an item consigned to us for auction, and then pulled out by the consignor before the auction, is subject to a penalty of twenty percent of the item's appraised value. It could cost you at least $200,000 or more to get your feathery back, Scott."

"That seems like a lot to pay for something I own, Jason."

"Yes, I know, but Covington Gallery has incurred expenses getting ready for the auction. Look, I have to report this to Sarah Covington in

London. She'll make the final decision as to the breach of contract issue. I'll call her and get back."

"Have you shipped the feathery to London?" Scott asked.

"Yes, we have, along with the bronze statuette of the golfer. They will leave this evening on a British Airways flight escorted by a courier. Covington Gallery's policy is to have any item valued as high as the feathery and the bronze hand-carried by a bonded courier."

"How about the rest?"

"They'll ship later by air freight."

"Sorry about this, Jason, but I feel like it's the right thing for me to do."

"Yes, Scott, but I only wish you'd decided to take back the feathery before we promoted it. The collectors are now clamoring to possess this long-lost relic, and it will be difficult to tone down their fervor." Gamby sounded disturbed on a personal note about Covington's loss of the feathery. "If we're finished here I'll ring up Sarah and inform her."

Matt got the gist of Scott's phone conversation with Gamby. "So, the feathery comes off the auction block?"

"Yeah, I think it's what Sandy would want instead of the feathery getting into the greedy hands of a Mario Carrabba or someone like him. I feel real good about being able to keep it, Matt. Scott expelled a deep breath and looked upward sayin; "Now the Feathery is mine and it's going to stay that way, Sandy."

"Done deal. Are you ready to talk about some tournament plans now?" Matt asked.

"Shoot."

"Suggest we leave for Scotland tomorrow and get a look at Turnberry before the British Open. It will give us ten days to practice, get used to the weather and get over jet- lag before the start."

"Sounds like a plan...book it, Matt."

The phone rang. Scott picked it up.

"Scott Beckman...Sarah Covington here. Straight away, I don't suppose I can talk you out of taking the feathery from the auction. I'm quite disappointed since I planned to bid on it myself."

Scott answered a voice that seemed disgruntled. "Sorry, I've made up my mind to keep it."

The phone was silent for ten seconds..."Gamby tells me you're a professional golfer on the tour. Are you playing in our Open at Turnberry?"

"Yes, I am."

"Could you stop over in London so we may sort out the contract issue?"

After a brief check with Matt, who'd just finished making their travel reservations, Scott answered her. "We have an overnight flight scheduled to arrive London on Tuesday morning, before we fly to Prestwick, Scotland on Wednesday. Could I meet with you some time on Tuesday in London?"

"That will be fine. You may come to the gallery around one in the afternoon, if that's all right." She gave Scott directions to the Covington Gallery in London.

AN UNDISCLOSED LOCATION

16

H is deep telephone voice came at her with a command. "I've sent my plane to pick you up. It will be there in one hour. I want you on board and on your way here."

She was used to his demands. They usually came sans explanation and she would respond in kind without question. After all, he paid her well. She packed a few things in a small leather carry-on and called the taxi that took her to the private plane terminal. The plane was there with engines running. After she boarded the sleek jet it was soon speeding down the runway and airborne.

When the Gulfstream V landed a limo was waiting on the ramp to whisk her to the meeting. It took place in his large Tudor style mansion. A butler escorted her to his viewing room where he sat in a swivel chair at a huge desk among other leather furniture. Persian carpeting covered the floor and display cabinets depicting antique golf memorabilia filled the room.

Without an offer of tea or indulging in small talk he gruffly explained the reason for his urgent beckon call. "My sources tell me that the McNair feathery ball has been removed from the auction in London."

"Oh, I'd not heard that," she said

"I pay you well to keep your ears and eyes open relative to my collecting thrust," he snarled. "As you know, I was going to out-bid all to possess that McNair feathery." He glared at her. 'Now, it's been pulled from the auction and we can't execute that plan."

"What now?" And she was sorry she asked, knowing anything she might say would trigger more of the ire stemming from his disappointment.

His answer came in a near scream. "I called you here to execute a recovery plan. He slammed his fist down on the mahogany desk. "You will obtain that feathery ball for me any cost."

She took a deep breath before asking the obvious question in support of his order.

"Where's the feathery at present?"

"My sources tell me that the feathery was being prepared for shipment from the Covington Gallery in New York City to London when the owner decided against auctioning it. It's either still in New York or on it's way by courier to London. In either case I want you to alert the New York and London people you've used before.

She was shaking when she asked. "Are the funds for this task available at the usual place?"

"Yes, I wired $500,000 to the Barkley Bank in your name." He stood up behind the desk and his eyes narrowed to stare at her. "I want that feathery ball in my collection!

Get it for me!

NEW YORK CITY

17

Detective Francis X. Riley was ordered to investigate a murder and attempted robbery at the Covington Gallery on Madison Avenue in New York City. He started to question one of the NYPD officers who'd first arrived at the crime scene. Riley squinted to read the officer's name tag. Straining to see small print signaled his need for glasses again. During a yearly physical the doc recommended bifocals. But the rugged forty-year-old detective thought glasses would detract from the image he wanted to present to bad guys. When the letters on the cop's name tag cleared he asked, "What've ya got, Grabowski?"

"The manager, Gamby, and some workers were preparing a shipment to England of some antique golf stuff." Officer Grabowski said. "A guy with a handgun burst into the room where they were packing the things."

"He came in through the Lobby?" Riley interrupted.

"Yeah, the guard on duty there must have tried to stop him and got shot."

***

After the coroner finished his work, one of his men zipped the guard's body into a rubber bag and they lifted it up on a gurney for transport to the morgue.

Riley knew the coroner, Dr. Jacob Stansfield. They'd met on many grim occasions like this one.

"A large caliber from something like a 357 went through his heart, tore up a lung and exited, making a big hole under his left shoulder blade, Francis." Dr. Stanfield said, and then added, "the forensic people have put the bullet in an evidence box."

"Can I take a look at the victim, Jake?"

The coroner unzipped the body bag halfway, and the face Riley saw wasn't just another homicide victim…It was Lem Shattuck's face. As a rookie he'd been assigned to partner with the veteran cop, and they'd become friends. After his assignment to homicide he would meet Lem occasionally at a Knicks game, have a fast beer afterwards and talk of old times. He'd lost track of Lem since attending his retirement party and figured he'd gone to Florida as planned.

The deep sigh from Riley was close to a sob as the coroner zipped the bag back over Lem's face. He got it back together after a few minutes and started doing what he was there for. "Did anyone ID the shooter?" he asked Grabowski.

"Best you talk to the manager, Mr. Gamby. He's in his office, detective."

Riley left the lobby and went to Gamby's office. He found Gamby sitting at his desk trying to regroup from the horror of what had happened. He removed both hands from his face and looked up at Riley. Riley introduced himself and flashed a wallet with his detective badge attached.

"I can't believe it.. Jesus, Joseph and Mary! He was going to retire at the end of the month. Lem was a loyal employee and my friend, detective."

"Mine too," Riley was quick to reply.

Riley's response that he was a friend of Lem confused Gamby, but he didn't question it, and in his present state of mind any explanation by the detective seemed unimportant.

Riley had his notebook and a pen in hand. "Tell me what happened here, Mr. Gamby."

Gamby started to put his hands to his face again, as if he wanted to hide from the vision he was recalling. "I was supervising the packing of a golf antique and memorabilia shipment to London when what sounded like a gunshot came from the lobby. A few seconds after, a masked man rushed into the room pointing a gun at us."

"What did the perpetrator look like?" Riley asked.

"A male, tall and heavyset. Over six feet, and I'd guess at least two hundred pounds. A ski mask covered his face...his eyes were glassy... wore a black leather jacket."

"What was he after, Mr. Gamby?"

"He wanted an item he thought was in the shipment we were preparing, but it was sent to our London gallery earlier today by courier."

"Then what?"

"He made a threat to blow my head off if I was lying about it being sent already. He rummaged through the shipment, ripping boxes open and cursing. After not finding what he was looking for, he left and ran toward the lobby."

"What's the item the guy was looking for, Mr. Gamby?" .

"The feathery."

Riley was confused. "What the hell is a feathery?"

"Oh, sorry. It's a rare, antique golf ball. Quite sought after by collectors."

Riley stared at Gamby, trying to understand how an old ball would be a reason to murder someone. After five seconds he expressed his shock in words spaced two seconds apart."A...golf...ball...Lem...Shattuck... was...killed...because...of...a...fucking...golf...ball?"

LONDON, UNITED KINGDOM

18

Six hours after leaving New York, the Boeing 777 approached Heathrow through fog and drizzle. The landing jolted Mike Edwards awake, and he looked out at the dank darkness of early morning England. As a courier, Mike made many trips, but most times he didn't know what was in the packages he carried in the leather case. This time it was different.

Gamby knew Mike was an avid golfer who lined up at four in the morning to play courses like Bethpage Black and others around New York City. Gamby had told him he was delivering a valuable antique feathery golf ball and a bronze statuette of a woman golfer.

Mike had read an article in a golf magazine about feathery golf balls. It explained that the USGA at Golf House in New Jersey ran a test on an ancient feathery ball comparing it to a modern one. They'd used a robotic driver at the same swing speed of 100 miles per hour for each drive. The result was that the feathery, made in the nineteenth century, was driven 178 yards compared to a distance of 240 yards for the modern ball. Mike was surprised that a golf ball filled with feathers and covered with leather could be driven only 62 yards less than a modern, high-tech golf ball. He would've liked to take a peek at the feathery, but the leather case was locked and sealed.

Mike presented the paperwork relating to the feathery and the bronze to a customs agent. When the antiques cleared, he proceeded to the terminal concourse where he handed the leather case to Bernard Brooks, an employee of Covington Gallery, who held a sign that read: MR. EDWARDS. The hand-off to Brooks completed Mike's courier task. In two hours he would be on a flight for his return to New York.

***

Two men lurking nearby watched the leather case change hands from Edwards to Brooks. They'd been tipped off on the arrival details of the feathery, and after observing the exchange they followed Brooks to the garage parking lot, virtually deserted in the early morning hour. When they caught up to Brooks, one of them grabbed the leather case and ran, while the other pulled a gun out of his jacket and aimed it at Brooks' chest. He fired just as Brooks brought up a kung fu kick at the gun. The gun was knocked out of the guy's hand, and it slithered across the cement floor, coming to rest under a parked car. The bullet smashed into Brooks' left shoulder, instead of his chest where it was aimed.

As Brooks lay injured on the garage floor, his assailant rushed to retrieve the gun. Just then the getaway car screeched to a stop, and the driver opened the passenger door frantically beckoning for his partner to get in. After he picked up the gun, the shooter ran to the car, and barely made it there before tires squealed a fast lurch toward the exit.

Brooks reached for his cell phone and touched the emergency numbers. He was able to ask for help and give his location before slipping into darkness.

19

An hour after Edwards' flight landed, Scott and Matt arrived at Heathrow. They retrieved their luggage and Scott's clubs, cleared customs and took a taxi to their hotel, not knowing one man was dead and another seriously wounded because of Scott's feathery and bronze statuette.

Shortly after they checked into the hotel, Scott left for the Covington Gallery to meet Sarah Covington. Matt planned to spend the morning strolling around London.

After a twenty-minute drive through the streets of London, Scott exited the taxi in front of a building made of granite and covered with ivy vines. He walked along the cobblestone pathway and up five pink marble steps. He opened a solid oak door and entered the Covington Gallery's foyer.

The receptionist picked up a phone and called Sarah Covington. After a few minutes she came down a corridor toward Scott. He'd expected an older lady and was surprised by her youth and beauty. Her ash blond hair was pulled back, with a few tendrils touching each side of her face. She walked up to him, held out her hand and grasped Scott's hand firmly. She didn't release it right away, and her green eyes looked into his with concern.

"Scott, I've just received some dreadful news." She told him about the killing at her New York gallery and the robbery and shooting at Heathrow.

Scott stood still with a blank expression on his face while the loss of the feathery and the bronze registered. But the killing of one person and the wounding of another over his golf antiques was much more difficult to grasp.

"Chief Inspector Bradshaw of Scotland Yard notified me of both events. He's in my office now. He has informed me that a homicide detective from New York City will arrive in London this evening. They suspect a link between the shootings here and in New York."

She led him down the hall to an office furnished with a large mahogany desk, a brown leather couch and two matching chairs. Chief Inspector Bradshaw sat in one of the chairs, and when they entered, Bradshaw's attention was on the floor-to-ceiling display cabinets covering the four walls. Three were filled with plaques and trophies with the name Sarah Covington embossed on each. The other cabinet featured old photos of St. Andrews and golf antiques and memorabilia that originated from there.

The chief inspector rose when they entered the room. "I've been admiring your many trophies," he said, "and I'm most interested in the Saint Andrews collection, Ms. Covington."

"Oh, thank you. It's only a small part of my private collection. I've a room full of many other golf collectibles. And most are from nineteenth century Saint Andrews."

She introduced Bradshaw to Scott. The distinguished gentleman was wearing a brown tweed sport coat with leather elbow patches. He came toward Scott. His thinning hair was cut short and had the same whiteness as his closely cropped beard. Scott thought Bradshaw fit Sherlock Holmes' description, even without the double-billed cap and curved clay pipe. They shook hands.

"Well, Mr. Beckman, your loss must be a dastardly blow."

"It is. But the killing in New York and shooting here are the worst part. How's the guy that got shot at Heathrow doing?"

"Mr. Brooks is in the hospital recovering. He's a tough army veteran, and his being an expert in hand-to-hand combat saved his life." Bradshaw continued, "I'm eager to interview him tomorrow since he should give me a fair description of the shooter and his accomplice."

"Who was killed at the Covington Gallery in New York?" Scott asked anxiously, "I know some of the people there."

"The guard, Lem Shattuck," Sarah answered.

Scott's hand went over his eyes. "Oh no, not him! I met the guy there. He was a retired cop trying to earn enough dough to retire in Florida and play golf. He wanted my autograph...Shit!"

"I knew him also," Sarah said. "I'm deeply saddened."

Scott took time to recover from learning about Lem Shattuck's death. "Any idea who did it?"

Bradshaw told Scott what he knew so far. "A Detective Riley from the New York City Police Department Homicide Division is investigating the murder and attempted robbery there. He's been told of the shooting at Heathrow. Mr. Gamby of Covington, New York informed him that a person by the name of Mario Carrabba was keenly interested in purchasing the feathery. Is that correct, Mr. Beckman?"

"Yes, I met with Carrabba before I contacted Covington Gallery."

"Would you please tell me about your meeting with Carrabba?"

Scott told Bradshaw about the low-ball offer for the golf antiques from Carrabba, the pressure from his so-called chauffeur, Rocco, and the disappointment Carrabba expressed during the phone call to tell him of his decision to auction the feathery with Covington.

"Detective Riley has interviewed Mr. Carrabba, and he'll brief me on that meeting when he gets here this evening, Mr. Beckman."

Scott got up from his chair to look at a painting of St. Andrews. It was a diversion to collect his thoughts. He sat back down and said, "I'm having trouble understanding the frenzy over the feathery ball. Two people being shot over it and the robbery. It just seems like a stretch."

"Mr. Beckman, I've seen this type of collector obsession create undue furor over a rare antique or work of art," Bradshaw said.

Scott accepted that statement coming from the chief inspector's experience, but something else about the robbery bothered him, and he voiced it. "Once they stole the feathery, wouldn't it be hot? I mean, they couldn't show it to anyone or put it on public display without getting caught and going to jail. I don't get it. Why would…?"

Bradshaw interrupted him. "It's not the nature of this type of beast to display their illicit booty. Our profiling of those who've stolen rare and valuable art or antiques shows they do it for self-gratification. They seldom flaunt their precious possession in front of others."

"So I wouldn't expect to see my feathery on TV's *Antique Road Show*?" Scott jibed.

Bradshaw chuckled. "No way. The culprit would just gloat over the fact he or she alone has possession of it."

Scott's arms went out, and the palms of his hands opened. This gesture toward Bradshaw asked for more of an explanation. "It just seems hard to believe murder would be involved."

"Not really, Mr. Beckman. It boils down to greed and possessiveness by a collector. They don't want anyone else to obtain what they've set their sights on."

Sarah reinforced Bradshaw's reasoning by saying, "Yes, I've experienced bitter competition during auctions, but murder does seem like an extremely exaggerated reaction."

The chief inspector tried to strengthen his point. "Consider the millions of pounds sterling or dollars some of the famous paintings by an artist like van Gogh have sold for at auction. If one of those paintings were eliminated from the auction at the last minute…well, you can imagine the frustration on the part of those with the original intent of obtaining it at any cost." The chief inspector paused for a moment before asking, "Why did you decide not to auction your feathery, Mr. Beckman?"

"Please call me Scott, sir. A teaching pro who was my mentor, Sandy McNair, left the feathery to me. He had no relatives when he died. Sandy helped me get through some tough times when I was a kid and taught me golf. His ancestors from Saint Andrews passed down the feathery to him, and I thought he'd want me to hold on to it. At first, I was reluctant to auction the feathery, but I needed money to stay on tour. After I started making cuts and earning prize money I decided to keep the ball."

The chief inspector wanted more detail. He asked Scott pointed questions about his trouble as a teen, the origin of the feathery in St. Andrews, Sandy McNair's ownership and the record round by Hugh McNair on the Old Course. His queries might have come from his interest in golf antiques and memorabilia more than to seek more background relating to the case at hand. A barrage of questions kept coming from Bradshaw.

After she checked the time on her wrist watch, Sarah Covington interrupted Bradshaw's request for more detail. "The McNair Journal, as part of Scott's collection, has an article written by a English newspaper reporter that tells of the record round, and more about the feathery." She looked at Scott. "If it's all right with you I can give the journal to the chief inspector for his review."

"Sure, if it helps his case, I'm all for it," Scott said.

Sarah left her office for a couple of minutes and returned with the McNair Journal. She handed it to Bradshaw. "I must caution you, Chief Inspector, this is a very valuable document."

"Why wasn't it sent with the feathery and the bronze?" Scott asked.

"Fortunately, Gamby, failed to send the journal with that same courier. When he informed me, I instructed him to send it with another courier straight away, and it arrived here a couple of hours ago."

Bradshaw put the journal in his briefcase. "Not to worry, Ms. Covington, I'm quite adept at taking good care of evidence, so this journal will be safe with me. "A collector who's determined to bid whatever it takes to obtain the feathery might still be driven by his or her obsession to possess it regardless of it being removed from the auction. That could be the motive for murder and robbery."

"How many collectors responded to the auction notice?" Scott asked.

Bradshaw looked toward Sarah Covington, who picked up a file folder from her desk. After counting the names. "There would've been twenty attending here in London and another ten tuned in to the closed-circuit presentation elsewhere ready to bid by phone. Many of those are just the curious. But according to past experience, only four of the collectors most interested in Saint Andrews golf antiques would be in the bidding competition at the end."

She handed the list of thirty names and addresses to Bradshaw. The four names she'd selected as the most interested collectors were underlined. In that group, there was a line drawn under the name Mario Carrabba.

Bradshaw scanned it quickly and cast his gaze toward a cabinet filled with Sarah's St. Andrews antiques. He grinned while saying, "Should I include you on this list, Ms. Covington?"

"In point of fact, Chief Inspector, I am keenly interested in the feathery, as well, but certainly not toward committing robbery and murder...really, sir!"

His smile faded as he changed the subject. "Ms. Covington, do you have any photographs of the feathery and the bronze statuette of the lady golfer?"

She opened the file folder again and handed him two color photos showing both antiques. "These were taken by our manager, Mr. Gamby, in New York before the shipment left."

Chief Inspector Bradshaw put the photos and the list of the collectors who planned to attend the auction in his briefcase. He got up to leave and made a slight bow to Sarah. "I'm off to a meeting in an hour with Detective Riley of the New York City Police Department." He shook Scott's hand. "Ms. Covington tells me you're scheduled to play in the Open. My very best wishes for your success there. Scotland Yard will do its best to recover your feathery and bronze lady golfer, and I look forward to apprehending those who acted so violently to possess them. I'll keep you informed of our progress. Are you staying at the Turnberry Hotel during the Open?"

"Yes, I am, sir. But I'm bummed out over the murder and robbery. Hope I can get it out of my mind so I can stay focused on my golf play at Turnberry."

"Good, I'll be in touch with you there. And Scott, if I'm to cease addressing you as Mr., please drop the *sir* on my behalf. One other suggestion...it's best for you to carry on with stiff upper lip and not dwell on what's happened. Scotland Yard will find the culprits and they'll be prosecuted. You're to go on with life...especially your pursuit of success at The Open.

***

Sarah returned to the office after escorting the chief inspector to the foyer. "Well, Scott, it's been a trying day for us both," she said.

Scott had turned away from inspecting her golf trophies when she entered. "You've won a lot of tournaments. Why did you quit?"

"After my mother died it was more of a leave of absence from the tour to straighten out the affairs of the gallery," Sarah explained. "At first I planned to take a year off to get it ready to sell, and I'd return to the tour after the sale was complete."

"And you ended up choosing a gallery full of antiques over playing golf?"

"Right. I became seduced by the antiques and decided to stay and manage it."

"I'd have to love something a lot before I'd quit the tour," Scott said, hesitating to gather his thoughts back to business concerns, but acting on Chief Inspector Bradshaw's suggestion to carry on despite the tragedies connected to his feathery, he asked. "What about the penalties involved in removing the feathery from the auction? And when will you auction the other things in the collection?"

Sarah looked at her watch. "I do want to talk to you about those issues, but I've an appointment right now. Could you wait for an hour until I finish meeting with some clients?"

Scott wanted to discuss the penalty issue with her instead of having it hanging over him in Scotland, so he agreed to wait. His sadness over Lem Shattuck's death and Brooks being injured was hard to shake off. He needed a diversion to keep from dwelling on those issues and thought viewing her antique golf collection might help. "You mentioned another room filled with your private collection of Saint Andrews golf antiques. Could I take a look? After reading McNair's journal I've become intrigued by St. Andrews golf in the old days."

"You certainly may, but if you don't mind, you'll have to look around there on your own."

20

Scott followed Sarah up a spiral stairway to a room on the third floor of the gallery, and she handed him a pair of white silk gloves. He recalled that Carrabba put gloves on before handling the feathery in Claudio's kitchen.

"It's okay to touch some of the items as long as you wear these, Scott." She hurried away, saying over her shoulder, "come down to my office when you finish."

He began to roam the room, impressed by the depth of Sarah's collection. The sheer volume of golf antiques squeezed into every nook and cranny suggested she'd seldom parted with many. There were antique golf clubs of every description, walking sticks and canes with old golf balls and club heads for handles, golf bags, clothing, books, postcards, paintings, scorecards, stamps, letters, photos, sculpture, silver, metalwork, trophies, glass, tableware, posters, beer steins, plates, pitchers, games and gutta-percha and feathery golf balls. Most of the items were connected to golf as it was played in the nineteenth century at St. Andrews.

Scott was interested in the feathery ball collection. Sarah had collected thirty of these superbly crafted balls made by Scots of the nineteenth century, such as Robertson of St. Andrews, Gourley and Alexander of Musselburgh and Marshall of Leith. Six of the feathery balls were marked with the name Hugh McNair of St. Andrews, but there wasn't a record score inked on them...only the pennyweight and the name Hugh on each ball.

Sarah also owned a large collection of gutta-percha golf balls. McNair's journal had enlightened Scott about these early golf balls made by Willie Dunn of Musselburgh and others. He'd read that the first gutta-percha golf balls were produced in 1848 and were not accepted until years later when improvements were made. The feathery ball-makers of Scotland were not privy to today's knowledge of ball flight and aerodynamics. They didn't know it was the stitching to close the bull hide leather cover that made the feathery fly better than the smooth-surfaced gutties. Later, it was the pattern of dimples on the gutta-percha ball that improved its flight, and the dimples came just in time for the first British Open in 1860.

The room contained a club made and probably used by Willie Park of St. Andrew's fame. As Scott gripped the driver he imagined Park might have used this very club when he'd won that first British Open at Prestwick, Scotland. His thoughts went to this year's British Open at Turnberry, Scotland, where he would soon compete.

Just as he was about to leave the room Scott noticed a small display case shrouded by a black cloth. He lifted the cloth. There was an item sitting alone inside the case. It was a narrow strip of stained maple wood with four recessed indentations. Three golf balls were on display there, resting in each of the three recesses, but the fourth one was empty. Under each ball, including the empty place, was a small gold plaque with letters inscribed on them in black.

He moved closer to the case and read the engraved names and numbers: AL GEIBERGER-59...CHIP BECK-59...DAVID DUVAL-59. They were familiar names as well as the record tournament scores made by each of those PGA players. He was surprised and somewhat puzzled when reading the inscription under the empty slot left for a fourth ball. The black letters on gold under that empty space spelled out the name HUGH McNAIR. It was followed by the number 78. Scott stared at the name and number quite some time before replacing the black cloth back over the glass case.

He spent over an hour examining the rest of the collection and left with much more to see. Scott hurried down the spiral stairway to Sarah's office, and when he entered, she was seated behind the desk typing on her computer keyboard.

"Any news from Scotland Yard?" he asked.

"Oh, hello, Scott." She swiveled her chair around toward him and smiled. "Nothing from Chief Inspector Bradshaw, but it's early in his investigation. Did you enjoy my Saint Andrews collection?"

"Yeah, it was real cool." Scott sat in a chair in front of her desk. "I saw the golf balls of Geiberger, Beck and Duval with their record scores of 59 beside them. Are they really the balls they used during those rounds?" Scott thought her grin before she answered was a weird one, and her face took on a slight blush.

"Oh, you uncovered that case?" Her attractive face changed to an ugly scowl of disapproval. "It was the ball those players finished their record round with." Her eyes narrowed and she sent him a strange look. There was a pause before she spoke again. "I expended an immense effort and great expense to acquire those golf balls. I'm sure you noticed the inscription under the missing ball." Again, her smile was more like a smirk.

"Yeah, I saw the empty slot for my McNair-78 feathery ball."

"Do you realize what it would mean to me to fill that fourth slot?" Sarah's inquiry sounded like a whine. And she answered her own question before Scott could. "I would have in my possession the balls played during the three record rounds in modern day golf, joined with the one used during a record round at Saint Andrews in the nineteenth century."

"A big deal and worth a lot of money, Sarah."

She glared at him with narrowed eyes. "Prestigious and priceless. It was a deep disappointment when you withdrew the feathery from my auction. You see, I was determined to outbid all the other collectors for it." She leaned forward with her elbows on the desk and gazed intensely at Scott. "My question to you, Mr. Beckman, is, If the McNair feathery is recovered, will you accept my offer of one million dollars for it?"

"I'm sorry. If I do get it back, I've still decided to keep it now that I can afford to."

It was like a cloud passed over her face before she forced a smile. "Very well. If the McNair feathery is recovered, I'll expect Covington Gallery to collect twenty percent of its appraisal value prior to auction. According to my barrister, the penalty for removing it from auction will be two-hundred thousand dollars."

Scott didn't possess the legal knowledge at hand to refute her threat, so he simply countered it with, "Whatever." Moreover, he thought her threat was deserving of that wise ass answer. "When will the other antiques in the collection be auctioned?"

"I plan to proceed with the auction as scheduled without the feathery and the bronze statuette. It will take place a week from today."

***

On their walk from her office to the lobby Sarah regained some of the congenial attitude she had before Scott denied her offer for the feathery. When they reached the door she held out her hand. "My very best wishes go to you during your play at the Open. I've some antique business there, and I'll be staying at my cottage in Portpatrick. I'll look you up in Turnberry."

Scott thought it was time to mention Matt. "My caddie used to work for you...Matt Kemp."

Sarah's congeniality suddenly disappeared. When she recovered she said, "oh, what a coincidence. He was very good, but I had to fire him."

"Why did you fire him if he was that good?" Scott asked.

Sarah hesitated for a moment. "He was spending too much time with an opposing player."

Scott's reaction to her reason was a blank stare. "Matt Kemp is an excellent caddie and my best friend."

She was silent after he said that. Scott took the hand she offered and left the gallery, relieved to be out of there. The cold rain falling in dark, dank London town fit well with his feelings about the sad news of today.

***

Matt enjoyed a lunch of fish and chips in a Trafalgar Square restaurant. The English specialty was served in a wicker basket lined with pages from Fleet Street tabloids. The newsprint carried stories of the infidelity and impropriety of naughty men and women from British royalty and parliament. It served the dual purpose of absorbing the grease from the fried fish and chips and obliterating some of those shocking revelations.

After his lunch, Matt entered a Barkley's Betting Shop. He'd been walking around enjoying the sights and sounds of London and decided to make a wager on the Open. The room was full of bettors hunched over their racing forms. Smoke from cigarettes as thick as a London fog made it difficult for them to clearly see the televisions displaying a variety of sporting events around the world.

Matt approached a clerk wearing a green visor who sat behind a caged enclosure and asked him for a British Open betting line. The clerk handed Matt a sheet with the odds beside each player's name. He skimmed down through the names on the list, ranging from the favorite to the long shot, Scott Beckman. The odds on Scott to win were at 200 to 1 as calculated by the Barkley odds-makers ten days before the tournament would start.

It didn't take long for Matt to make his bet. He told the clerk, "Five hundred pounds to win on Scott Beckman at the British Open."

Matt passed the money through a space under the cage, and the clerk repeated the bet with a bewildered expression on his face. The dismay came because the Yank in front of him was wagering the equivalent of 880 United States dollars on a virtually unknown golfer to win a major golf tournament...the bloody British Open. The clerk's look at Matt was askance when he handed him the betting slip saying, "good luck, mate."

***

When Matt returned to the hotel room he struggled with the idea of making a call, but finally picked up the phone and dialed a London number on a small paper he'd kept in his wallet for a long time.

"Hello, Jennifer Lawton."

"Matt, is that you? Where are you?"

"In London. Can you make it for dinner tonight?"

There was a pause. "Oh, Matt, I'm trying to sort things out with a friendship I'm in, and the timing for us to get together is just not right. It's a lady friend who sponsored me when I first started on tour. She would like to move in with me. I don't want that. I'm meeting with her tonight to explain and try to remain her friend. "

Matt didn't want his disappointment to show, so he changed the subject. "Are you still on the European tour?"

"Yes, but I've qualified to play on the LPGA in America. I'm leaving for there in a fortnight. Want a job?"

"No thanks. I'm employed and headed for the Open with a good player and best friend."

"Great, good luck there. Are you coming back through London on your way home?"

"Yes, I am."

"Good, I would like to see you then. It'll be a better time than now." She paused again. "Matt, I've never forgot us."

"Me neither, Jennifer. I'll see you here in London in about two weeks."

"Always, Matt."

After she said that, there was a click and the call ended. Matt held the phone for ten seconds while staring at the ear piece.

***

Matt was stretched out on a twin bed watching golf on the BBC when Scott entered the room. "Long meeting at the gallery? How's the wicked witch of the East?"

"About the same as you described her. And you're not going to believe what's come down in the last twenty-four hours." He told Matt about the murder in New York and the shooting and robbery at Heathrow.

When Scott finished, Matt shook his head. "Man, the gallery guard in New York gets killed over the Feathery. A real bummer. And that bronze statue of the lady golfer went with the feathery?"

"Yeah, but the police here think the robbery and murder were all for the feathery."

Matt's concern showed. "But the loss of that statuette cuts into your future bankroll, doesn't it?"

"Right, but we've got enough to play Turnberry. And the money from Covington's auction of the other stuff next week will keep us in a few more tournaments even if I miss the cut at the Open."

"Hey, I'm betting you'll not only make the cut, but win the damn thing." Matt reached in his shirt pocket and handed Scott a small piece of paper, saying, "You're in for half of this."

Scott looked at the betting slip, shook his head, and said, "five hundred pounds on me to win at 200 to one? You are one crazy dude." His smile was the first in hours.

21

I'm having trouble coming to grips with why a person would commit murder and attempt to kill someone else over a golf ball!" New York City Detective Francis X. Riley, said while trying to subdue his Brooklyn accent in front of a group of proper English speaking inspectors. He was seated at a conference table in Scotland Yard headquarters, and included in the group of inspectors were three representatives from the Yard's Art and Antique Squad. Riley was in London following his initial investigation of a murder at Covington Galleries in New York City.

"But, Detective Riley, this isn't *just* a golf ball," replied Chief Inspector Trevor Bradshaw in his clipped accent. "This is *the* golf ball, the feathery, the Holy Grail of golf balls. This is the ball Hugh McNair shot an astounding 78 with at Saint Andrews in 1849. A record score then, and perhaps the equivalent of a 58 that would break the current record of 59 set in our primary modern golf tournaments."

"What kinda money we talking about?"

"Priceless, detective."

"Priceless? A golf ball?"

"To put it in perspective, what would the first baseball Babe Ruth hit for a home run be worth?"

Riley shook his head. "Hard to say."

"I read recently, Detective Riley, that Ruth's bat, the one he used to hit the first home run in your Yankee Stadium, sold at auction for over one million dollars. Now, imagine if you owned both the first and last home run balls Babe Ruth hit. Well, baseball started in your country and its been adopted as a national pastime, so those baseballs would be dear to American collectors, but golf started here, and is our national pastime. In point of fact, the game has spread over much of the world, so perhaps this feathery has a broader value worldwide than those Babe Ruth baseballs." Bradshaw gave an inquisitive glance. "Do you have my point, Detective Riley?"

Riley nodded slowly. And those seated around the table looked at one another for a moment before an inspector sitting next to Riley broke their silence. "So where do we begin, Chief Inspector?"

"After lunch I'll brief you all on the history of this feathery golf ball and how we'll proceed with the investigation. Detective Riley will report on his interview with a person of interest in New York City by the name of Carrabba.. We shall recess and return here in two hours. During my lunch I'll read a newspaper article written in 1849 for background. It's part of a journal put together by Hugh McNair and tells about his record round on the links of Saint Andrews while playing with this feather and leather ball of antiquity fame."

The inspectors seated at the table knew Bradshaw's briefings relating to golf memorabilia and antiques were never brief because the history of the game of golf was his hobby. Their hope was that the article in the journal might move the afternoon session along more rapidly.

***

The inspectors with Detective Riley left the building and headed to the local pub for lunch. Bradshaw entered his office. He went to a safe, spun the combination dial a few times, and removed the McNair Journal. He put on a pair of latex gloves, sat down at his desk, and propped the journal up on a book-stand, then took a ham sandwich out of a brown bag and poured a cup of tea from a thermos. His habit of adeptly handling evidence and the like while eating lunch was his rare breach of Yard protocol...a flamboyant and purposeful departure from the discipline imposed by his office. Even though the journal was not evidence but a valuable antique document, this divergence and time saving habit was retained.

Bradshaw searched the journal pages until he located an article written by Alistair Beddington in 1849. He put his feet up on the desk, took a bite from the sandwich in his left hand while turning the pages with his right.

***

They were all seated at the conference table when Bradshaw entered. He said, "I've just read an amazing article in the McNair Journal written in 1849, loaned to me by the owner of the feathery. I was able to complete reading a description of how the now purloined ball was manufactured in McNair's shop in 1849 and used during a record round at St. Andrews.

Bradshaw sat in a chair at the head of the table and placed some notes scribbled on a yellow pad in front of him He said, "I'll brief you all on the construction of the famous ball and the record round as told in the article. It will be worthwhile background for all working this case."

After almost an hour into Bradshaw's not so brief-briefing, Riley interrupted. "With all due respect, Chief Inspector, I think we've enough background on this feathery ball. I'd like to get on to something else."

"Quite, Detective Riley. Sorry, I sometimes get carried away when the case involves golf antiques and memorabilia. He nodded toward Riley. "You have our attention. Tell us about this American chap, Carrabba.

Riley squinted at his notes and then reluctantly reached in his briefcase for his new prescription glasses. He put them on, still feeling self-conscious about the middle-aged stigma attached. Riley peered down at the yellow legal pad in front of him,and started his brief.

"When I arrived at the golf course, owned by Carrabba near Saratoga, New York, the security guard at the gate informed me he was playing out on the course. The starter gave me a golf cart and I was directed to the seventeenth where I caught up with Carrabba's foursome. He greeted me with only a nod and mumbled a request that I follow them down the eighteenth to the clubhouse."

Riley continued, "His playing partners looked familiar. Most likely because the three of them were parolees and underworld-connected. Their mug shots were circulated for years around NYPD precincts. There was a fifth member of the group, but he wasn't playing. Rocco Vitale drove the golf cart for Carrabba. I recognized him as a perp I'd arrested for assault and possession of cocaine when I worked the narcotics division before transferring to homicide. Vitale is also suspected of several gang murders.

"Rocco has an extensive rap sheet, initiated at age fourteen, and has done time. He must've recognized me based on the sour look he sent my way. Rehabilitation programs in prison hadn't made him an honest man. That was evident when I saw Rocco kick his boss' golf ball from deep grass onto the fairway. It went unnoticed by the other players, who I later found out were playing in something called a five hundred dollar Nassau match."

One of the inspectors who played golf smiled and said, "this Rocco bloke has no respect for the integrity of the game." He then asked,

"Where was Rocco when the guard was shot at the gallery in New York, detective?"

"When we reached the clubhouse which, by the way, has two rooms full of golf antiques and memorabilia, I asked that question. The answer I got was that Rocco was in Las Vegas with his boss, Carrabba. A few phone calls verified their alibi."

"Do you still consider Mario Carrabba and his associates as persons of interest?" Bradshaw asked.

Before he answered Bradshaw, Riley made a point while adding some humor. " I believe the term, 'persons of interest', originated in your country, Chief Inspector. We still call them 'suspects' where I come from. Like in 'round up the usual suspects.' It wouldn't have sounded right to Bogie if the inspector in the movie *Casablanca* said to his men, 'round up the usual persons of interest,' now, would it?"

Bradshaw seemed a little disturbed by Riley's discourse on semantics, but sent a wry smile his way and said, "probably not. How about Carrabba?"

"Carrabba wants to own the feathery at any cost, and he's well connected in New York. I suppose he could've hired someone to go after it for him. I did find out he'd made reservations to attend the auction at Covington Gallery here in London. I think he should remain a suspect."

"How about ballistics on the bullet used in the New York Gallery murder?" An inspector asked.

Riley handed the enlarged photos of the round taken from that crime scene to Bradshaw and pointed to the bullet. "The bullet that killed my friend Shattuck came from a 357 Magnum."

Bradshaw opened the folder, and raised an eyebrow. "The bullet we retrieved from the garage at Heathrow is from a 38 caliber."

"Not a match," Riley said. "Did your interview with the victim at Heathrow get you a description of the shooter and his accomplice? By the way, that's a hell of a kick the guy made."

"Yes, Detective Riley, Brooks is quite efficient at martial arts, you know. Served twenty years in British Special Forces."

"The description?" Riley asked again.

"Oh yes. The shooter is almost two meters tall and weighs about fourteen stone. The getaway car driver and the one who snatched the case with the feathery ball and the bronze is a head shorter and a lightweight."

The inspector sitting next to Riley saw a look of confusion cloud over Riley's face. He made a meter to foot and stone to pound conversion. "The shooter is approximately six-feet-two- inches and one-hundred-ninety pounds, detective Riley."

Bradshaw continued, "Seems like the one who had the gun kicked out of his hand spoke with an Irish brogue."

The chief inspector's statement got the attention of three inspectors seated at the table. They were working on a case involving corruption in a gambling network that had linkage to the Irish Republican Army.

***

After the meeting, Bradshaw invited Riley to his office. He sat in the chair behind his desk with his feet propped up beside a stack of case files. Bradshaw opened a drawer and took out the list of golf auction high bidders Sarah Covington had given him. Listed and underlined along with Mario Carrabba were the names Jaspar Johncke, Ian Barkley and Mary Harding. He handed the list to Riley.

"So these are the high rollers?" Riley asked.

"Yes. They're the prime collectors, and they've a history of bidding high to obtain golf antiques. All four planned to attend auction of the feathery before it was stolen. I consider these four persons of interest because their craving to own the feathery could've continued after it was eliminated from the auction."

Riley looked down the list and saw the name Sarah Covington added to it.

"Who's that?" Riley asked.

"She's the owner of Covington Gallery, the auction house."

"Suspect?"

"Not a strong suspect, more of a person of interest." He smiled at Riley before saying, "you see, Detective Riley, therein lies the difference between the two terms."

"Okay, okay, but why is she on your list?"

Ms. Covington was going to bid on the feathery. Her desire to possess it is strong, so I shan't rule her out just now. His notebook was on top of the desk in front of Bradshaw. He reviewed the notes made during interviews with Scott and Sarah Covington and shared them with Riley. Then he wrote at the top of a blank page in his notebook the name

Ian Barkley. "We have an appointment with Barkley at his home this evening."

"Whoa! Who's this Barkley guy who needs a house-call instead of coming to Scotland Yard?" Riley asked.

"He's a multimillionaire who owns one hundred and fifty betting shops across Britain, Wales, Ireland and Scotland. Barkley never leaves his mansion. He runs his gambling empire from his computer-laden home. A background check told us he was once an avid golfer but was asked to resign from The Belfry Club because of his cheating in money matches."

"He sounds like the character, *Goldfinger*, in that old James Bond movie. Would Barkley kill for the feathery?" Riley asked.

"He's very determined to acquire that most rare find. Barkley knows everyone in golf antique collecting circles," Bradshaw added. "Even if he's not implicated, Barkley might lead us to those who are."

Riley got up to leave. "Can't wait to meet the infamous Mr. Barkley."

"I'll pick you up at your hotel at four o'clock this afternoon, and you'll have that distinct pleasure, Detective Riley."

22

The chief inspector picked up Riley in front of his hotel and settled into Bradshaw's Audi for the short ride to South Kensington for their meeting with Ian Barkley.

They drove into the circular driveway in front of Barkley's Tudor-style mansion and parked near the entrance. Bradshaw pressed the doorbell, and a faint ringing sound could be heard from the other side of a thick wooden door. The man who opened it had scarred eyebrows and cauliflower ears. Those flaws told his past occupation to Riley, but he thought the altercations causing them may not have been governed by rules set down by the Marquis of Queensbury. Riley also observed a telltale bulge on his leather jacket that could have been a shoulder holster snuggling a handgun inside it.

The short, compact man told them in an Irish brogue, "I'm Malachy. Mr. Barkley will see you gentlemen upstairs in the communication center."

They followed the short man's limp up two flights of a spiral staircase. A sequence of numbers punched by Malachy on a keyed entry system opened the door into what he told them was Barkley's viewing room.

They were ushered in to a huge chamber that could've been a spacious library at one time, but now it was a museum filled with golf antiques. The high ceiling held an immense crystal chandelier in the center that was set to low luminescence in deference to spotlights aimed strategically to play up the contents of several display cabinets. Bradshaw lingered behind Riley and Malachy, intent on getting a glimpse of the 150-year-old golf clubs, golf balls and memorabilia dedicated to the game of golf as it was played in the nineteenth century.

Malachy noticed Bradshaw lagging behind them admiring the Barkley collection and said, "Mr. Barkley spends hours alone in here looking at these things."

The chief inspector nodded knowingly. Malachy's remark validated the point he'd made earlier that collectors of rare antiques were prone to spend hours in solo admiration of their relics.

They followed Malachy as he keyed in the combination to another door leading from Barkley's museum, down a short hallway to his gambling control center. It was a fast transition for Riley and Bradshaw from ancient golf to a room filled with modern technology. The room was packed with computers and satellite television monitors. The displays showed horse races and other sporting events throughout Europe. Some of the computers seemed to be calculating profit-and-loss from wagers in real time within each betting shop in the Barkley network.

Malachy led them through this maze of electronic wizardry to Barkley, who was hunched over a keyboard in front of a master control panel. His short neck had three deep wrinkles in the back leading down to his rounded shoulders. The neck barely separated Barkley's shiny bald head from that shoulder slump. Riley was not as grossed out by those features as he was by the fact that Barkley's rotund body was stark naked.

Barkley's index fingers were busy typing commands into his gambling network. Riley was mesmerized as he watched him bring up wagering results with bottom line numbers showing astounding totals.

Just as Bradshaw's irritation over being ignored was about to erupt, Barkley made the last entry into his conglomerate of betting shops. He reviewed the results, and exited the program. He spun his chair around to face his visitors and said, "and what can I do for you, Chief Inspector?"

Bradshaw's blue eyes squinted to narrow. "First off, get dressed and out of the all together. Secondly, I came here in deference to your aversion to leaving this mansion. I presume I'll be able to get the information I need. If not, you'll have to leave here for a visit to Scotland Yard. Do we have an understanding, sir?"

Barkley gazed at Bradshaw with an expression of surprise, then the fear of leaving his fortress for the outside world played on his face. Malachy was ready with a blue silk robe, and Barkley slipped his arms into it and tied the belt with a flourish.

"Please come with me to the conference room." Barkley said. "I'll give you my full attention for as long as you require it."

Bradshaw introduced Riley, but Barkley ignored Riley's hand, explaining he didn't shake hands to avoid germs being transferred through physical contact.

Barkley gave refreshment orders to Malachy before they followed him through a labyrinth of corridors to a luxurious conference room. They sat down at a table large enough to accommodate twenty people. Malachy returned with a serving tray that offered a selection of tea, coffee and scones.

Bradshaw began. "The Yard has assigned me to investigate a shooting and the armed robbery of a valuable feathery golf ball and bronze statuette. Detective Riley is here to determine if there's a link between a murder in New York and the robbery here. Since you are renowned in golf antique collecting circles, we're hopeful you may be able to help us."

"I'll assist you in any way I can." Barkley said. "You see, I gave up playing golf years ago. Now, it's my passion to own the rarest of golf antiques. I'd like to acquire that feathery ball if it's recovered. And I was willing to bid as high as three million pounds for it at the Covington Gallery auction before it was removed by the owner."

Bradshaw tried not to look impressed. "There's something I'd like to ask you straight away, Mr. Barkley."

"Go right ahead, Chief Inspector."

"Do you know a Swedish gentleman named Jaspar Johncke?"

"Of course. He was a colleague of mine and a leading golf antique collector."

The chief inspector was taken aback by his answer. "*Was* a colleague of yours? Are you no longer associates?"

"It isn't that at all, sir. Johncke passed away in Sweden only last week. He had a history of heart trouble, and unfortunately did not take very good care of himself. He visited me here just a few weeks before his death."

Bradshaw was surprised to hear that Johncke was dead. He was, after all, one of his prime persons of interest. He asked, "what business did you have with Mr. Johncke on his visit here?"

"We were rivals in collecting golf antiques, and Johncke outbid me for rare items several times. He was always offering to buy some of mine."

"How do you know he died?" Bradshaw asked.

"I was informed of Jaspar's passing by his barrister. We had some business pending, and he rang me up with the news. Why do you ask?"

"Mr. Johncke's name came up during the investigation, and I wondered about your connection with him."

"You don't think Jaspar was involved in the robbery, do you?" Barkley asked and then gave his own answer. "That's impossible, the man was a multimillionaire."

"He was a person of interest like you and some other millionaires because of their zealous interest in obtaining the feathery. We believe that interest could've continued after the feathery was removed from the auction," Bradshaw added. He looked at Barkley for a reaction but got none. Then he asked, "Did Johncke mention the feathery during his visit?"

"Yes, and I put him on notice that I'd outbid him for it, and the McNair feathery was destined to be mine." Barkley grinned at them.

Bradshaw took his yellow note pad out of his briefcase. "I have a few more questions to ask you."

"Proceed."

"Have you had the so-called McNair 78 feathery in your possession at any time?"

"No."

"Do you have any information as to the whereabouts of the McNair feathery?"

"No."

There was a pause before Riley said, "I'd like to ask your..." he searched for the right words among body-guard, servant and butler before deciding on "employee, Malachy, a few questions."

Barkley summoned Malachy back to the conference room.

"Malachy, what's your last name?" Riley said, beginning the questioning.

"Gallagher," he answered.

"Place of birth?"

"Belfast, Ireland."

"When were you at Heathrow last?"

"Christmas Eve, four years ago for a flight to Belfast to see my mum."

"Were you there this past Tuesday morning?"

"No."

"Is that a gun under your coat?"

Barkley jumped in on the question. "This man's duty is to protect me, and I've obtained a permit for his weapon."

"May I see the gun?" Riley asked.

Barkley nodded. "All right, but I don't understand the implication."

Malachy reached inside his coat and handed the gun to Riley. Riley noted that the safety was on, and there was a round in the chamber. He cleared the round and sniffed at the end of the barrel. His sniff indicated it hadn't been fired recently, unless it had been thoroughly cleaned afterward.

"May I have a word with you outside the room?" Riley asked Bradshaw.

They left the conference room and walked down a corridor.

"It's a 38. Same type of gun that fired the bullet that hit Brooks." Riley handed the gun to Bradshaw. "We need ballistics to check it out, and I suggest Brooks have a look and a listen at Malachy Gallagher."

"Righto, I'll ask Gallagher to accompany us to the hospital. And the lab will fire a bullet from Malachy's gun and look for a match with the one taken from Brooks' shoulder."

After their corridor sidebar, Bradshaw and Riley returned to the conference room and informed Malachy about his pending trip to Scotland Yard. Barkley seemed relieved that he wouldn't have to leave his gambling citadel to accompany Gallagher into the outside world.

Bradshaw spoke curtly to Barkley in parting. "If you hear anything about the feathery circulating among your fellow collectors or about anyone trying to fence it, call me."

The chief inspector handed Barkley his card, and they escorted Malachy through the mansion, outside and into the backseat of the Audi.

TURNBERRY, SCOTLAND

23

Scott and Matt left London at nine in the morning and landed in Prestwick, Scotland, a little over an hour later. Inspired by his inheritance of the golf antiques, Scott read a book on the flight over about the history and tradition of golf in nineteenth century Scotland. When they touched down for his first visit to Scotland his thoughts went to the early legends who played and made a business out of the game of golf. Scotland was the home of Old Tom and Young Tom Morris, Willie Park, the Dunn twins, Robert Forgan, Allan Robertson, John Gourlay, and a man he'd become familiar with of late by the name of Hugh McNair.

Eager to play a round of golf, they quickly left the airport and drove the rented Land Rover into the Prestwick Golf Course car park. They'd continue on toward Turnberry later. The book he read on the plane noted that the course had been host to the first British Open in 1860 and more Open championships that followed on these venerable links. Willie Park had won the first, and both Tom Morrises had prevailed there after.

They walked Prestwick, a course not much changed since the 1800s. The play there brought Scott's thoughts away from the aftermath of the murder and robbery. Studying each lie, selecting the right club and determining the line for a putt brought back some logic and order that'd been knocked aside by those horrible events.

***

After leaving Prestwick they drove south along a narrow shore road to Turnberry. The British Open would start in nine days. They were there earlier than the other players, who would begin arriving in a week. Scott talked over his plan for practice with Matt. He'd dedicate three hours a day on the range and putting green, and play the course at least eight times before the tournament began. The available time to play and practice would be extended by the daylight of Scottish summertime, lasting until ten in the evening.

They drove up to the Turnberry Hotel overlooking both the Arran and Ailsa championship courses. It was a rambling Victorian-era building, white with a red tile roof, a railroad hotel constructed in the early twentieth century when trains brought golfers to enjoy the course and the luxury of the grand hotel.

When they reached the hotel entrance, Matt said, "I won't be staying here."

Scott was puzzled. "Why not?"

"We Sherpas have our own place."

"Where do the caddies stay, Matt?"

"It's called the Kilt and Jeans Inn and Pub. Good food and beer, with lovely ladies hanging out there."

"Okay, I understand. I'll drop you off there after you show me the course."

Scott checked into the hotel, and afterwards they visited the pro-shop where he met the head professional, Derrick Small. Derrick was a blond, heavyset man at six-foot-three. They shook hands. Derrick's hand covered all of his, and it occurred to Scott that Derrick's golf clubs must require a few extra layers of tape under the grips to accommodate those large mitts. Derrick welcomed Scott's early arrival. He gave him permission to play the course and to use its practice facilities.

Matt drove the golf cart to the first tee of Ailsa course and stopped there for Scott to get his first look at it. It was easy to observe the whole panorama from there since the course was void of any trees to block the view.

"I've caddied here twice and know this course pretty well." Matt said. "It plays at a total yardage of 6998...par 71. It's nothing like the *target*-type golf courses you're used to in the States, Scott. The rough is knee high and the bunkers are deep. The strategy here is to keep the ball on the fairway, and those deep pot-bunkers out of play. You should let the driver stay in your bag on most holes and use irons off the tee. It's a position golf game here with a lot of bump-and-run shots to the green instead of high-flying approach shots."

Scott was taking it all in. "Hey Matt, the fairways look burned out. What are those tall flowers in the rough? Whoa, stop here. That bunker's so deep, it has a ladder for a player to climb in and out."

"It's rare to play here on green grass fairways," Matt said. "Those posies are called heather with wire-like stems that grab at the shaft of your club on the down swing. Most players who get into that bunker with the ladder must come out of it hitting a sideways shot instead of going directly for the green."

"This is going to take some getting used to. Glad we're here early."

"Welcome to links golf at the British Open, dude." Matt drove on.

Scott looked over at some adjacent fairways. "Is that the other course over there?"

"Yeah, it's called the Arran, and it'll be a parking lot during the Open."

The cart moved slowly up the first fairway as Matt continued to narrate the tour. "The first hole runs toward the Firth of Clyde. That's the Irish Sea..." Matt's wave followed the curved shore line of Turnberry Bay.

As they turned to the second tee, Scott looked out on the water. In the distance he saw a large black hill of an island that rose above the Firth of Clyde, and it dominated the horizon for miles around. He remembered it was one of the many geographical features near golf courses Sandy told him about. Sandy said it looked like the rock of an island at Morro Bay in California, only it was much larger.

Matt noticed him staring out at the mammoth lump of granite rising from the sea. "That's Ailsa Craig. The locals tell me the island is most always covered in clouds."

"Well, we can see it today. Hope it stays that way."

"It won't. The Scots that live along these shores say 'if ye can't see the Ailsa Craig it's raining. If you can see it, it's *aboot* to rain.' The Ailsa Craig is home to thousands of gannets. The white sea birds come from there to dive into the water here after fish." Matt pointed toward Turnberry Bay. "The gannets are not bothered by bad weather...they love it. Golfers who play well in the wind and rain here are called *gannets* by the locals."

"If the weather here gets bad I'd want to be called a *gannet*." Scott was checking the course score card as they drove along. "What do these weird names for each hole mean?"

"All the holes here at Turnberry have names telling a special feature, view, or hazard. Like *Mak Siccar* in Scottish is 'Make Sure', as well as *Lang Whang* for the longest hole. The ninth tee hangs over a rocky ledge and drops off fifty feet to the water." Matt pointed out the Turnberry

Lighthouse in the distance and a stone pillar, or cairn, that'd been placed two hundred yards out in the center of the fairway, serving as a target for the driven golf ball to fly over. "This course was made into an airfield during World War Two, and was restored afterwards. A monument is here to honor those fliers who didn't make it back to Turnberry after their mission."

As they drove along, Matt showed Scott the best positions on the golf course to land a ball for his next shot and told him about the tricks of certain greens, pointing out the best approach to them. The weather was calm now, but he warned Scott of the potential for gale and driven rain that could suddenly come off the sea to alter such tranquility and change Turnberry's character from serene to ugly.

After inspecting the course, they were on the putting green and driving range for three hours. Scott drove Matt to the Kilt and Jeans Inn and Pub. After Matt checked in, they had a beer at the bar, a traditional watering hole for caddies working the Open at Turnberry.

***

When Scott returned to his room at the hotel, he placed a call to Beth Sweeney in New York. He brought Beth up to date on what he'd been up to since they'd last talked and told her about the robbery and murder.

"No way, Scott," she said. "That feathery ball is dangerous to one's health."

Beth mentioned she'd passed the New York bar exam and had been hired by a Manhattan firm dealing with international issues. Ever since his London meeting with Sarah Covington, Scott was concerned about not having representation during the auction of the antique items, minus the feathery and bronze. Also, Sarah's threat to penalize him $200,000 was still hanging over his head.

"Hey, Beth, could you represent me at an auction in London next week?" Scott filled her in on the details of the auction and the penalty imposed on him if the feathery was recovered.

"I'm new in the firm, but I'm sure they'll let me go. That penalty by Covington should be negotiable. What about insurance?"

"That's the kicker. If the feathery and bronze are not recovered, the insurance policy bought by Covington should cover the loss, and I'd be compensated for the value of those items. Then Covington would still try to take the two hundred thousand penalty from the insurance settlement amount because I removed the feathery from the auction. If the feathery *is* recovered, and I don't submit it to an auction by Covington, I'm still liable for the penalty according to Covington. It's a catch-22."

"How about the value of the bronze and the penalty relative to it?" Beth asked.

"I didn't remove the bronze statuette from the auction, just the feathery, so there's no penalty on the bronze. However, now I want to keep it, too."

"Okay, Scott, I think I understand."

"It's too complicated for this golfer but it should be a piece of cake for you legal beagles, right?"

"I'll give it my best, Scott."

"Thanks. I feel better about it now."

"I hope you feel the same when you get our bill." She laughed.

Scott paused a moment, then asked, "Could you come over to Turnberry, Scotland, after the auction in London? It'd be at my expense."

"You mean for the British Open?" She asked.

"Right."

"Wow, I'll try it on the partners and let you know about both London and that."

"I'll look forward to having you here, Beth"

They said their good-byes. Scott cradled the phone and then picked it up quickly on impulse to call his mother in San Diego and invite her to the Open. Before he thought more about her sour attitude about golf, he made the call. Her secretary put his call through immediately.

"Is that you Scott? Oh, how I've waited for you to call. Had no idea where you were."

"I'm in Scotland, mom. I'll be playing in the British Open next week. Do you want to come over for it?"

Diane Beckman paused before she answered. "I can't, Scott."

"Have you got another big real estate deal in the way, mom?"

"No, not at all. I have two appointments with the psychiatrist next week, and we're making so much progress, I don't want to interrupt it."

"Progress?" Scott asked.

"Yes, I'm coming to grips with my problems relating to losing your dad, my relationship with you, and if you can believe it, even my resentments about the game of golf."

"Wow, that is progress. Do you know what caused all that?"

"It started before Zachary was killed, but that escalated it. I selfishly resented the amount of time he spent with you on the golf course. I was bitter about you, and he not taking part in my love of tennis. I took a lot of that out on your dad and you after he died."

"Okay, mom. It's important that you continue those sessions. Sounds like you're almost through sorting it all out. I'll see you in a couple of weeks."

"I'll be watching on television. Good luck, Scott, and make a lot of birdies. Bye. I love you and I'm proud of you."

Scott put down the phone and tears filled his eyes. Her last words were ones he'd never heard her say...*birdies, I love you, and I'm proud of you.*

The situation with his mother had been hanging over Scott for years, and it was a huge relief for him to feel it could finally be improving. It took five minutes before he could clear the emotions connected to her last words.

The stolen feathery and unsolved murder and robbery was nagging at him. He thought he'd better put it out of his mind and concentrate on preparing for the Open and leave it up to Chief Inspector Bradshaw and Scotland Yard to solve the crime. He spoke to the empty room. "I'm a professional golfer, not a detective."

LONDON

24

Two days after their visit with Ian Barkley, the betting shop mogul, Bradshaw was waiting for Riley to arrive at his Scotland Yard office. The detective was returning to New York that evening, and the purpose of their meeting was to review progress on the case. While waiting for Riley to arrive he munched on a ham sandwich while reading some of the other articles compiled by McNair in his journal. He was informed by his secretary of Riley's arrival. He quickly placed the half eaten ham sandwich in a desk drawer, took off the gloves and returned the journal to his safe before Riley entered the office.

After greeting Riley, Bradshaw referred to a page in one of his yellow notepads taken from the same desk drawer where half of his ham sandwich hid from scrutiny by Riley. Circles were drawn on the pad with the names of his persons of interest inside them. Lines with arrows connected the circles to his comments at the bottom of the page: COLLECTOR; ROBBER; MURDERER or FENCE. Bradshaw passed the pad across the desk to Detective Riley, who sat in a chair across from him.

"Your investigation of Carrabba and his ensuing alibi has all but eliminated him from the list. Still, it would be well for you to keep an eye on Mr. Carrabba when you return to New York, Detective Riley."

Riley studied Bradshaw's matrix. The names Ian Barkley, Mary Harding, Mario Carrabba and Jaspar Johncke were there. "Barkley's man, Malachy Gallagher, checked out okay. Brooks said he bears no resemblance to the guys who snatched the feathery at Heathrow. Your ballistics experts told me Gallagher's gun isn't the one that shot Brooks. But your people tell me they're interested in the Irishman, Gallagher, for some past crimes connected to the IRA."

"Righto, and Scotland Yard is investigating Malachy Gallagher's activity while associated with Barkley, who's under scrutiny for some illegal gambling business."

Riley looked down at Bradshaw's notebook again, and pointed a finger at the name, Johncke, the Swede, who, according to Barkley, had died. "Why is Johncke still listed here?"

"We've found he had a history of having others do the dirty work of convincing antique collectors to give up what they cherished."

"So you think Johncke could have been involved in both the New York murder and Heathrow robbery?"

Bradshaw paused before he answered Riley. His eyes were locked onto a name on the list. "It's a possibility, but there's another who could've been a co-conspirator."

"How and who?" Riley asked.

"This person of interest has worked with Johncke on other occasions to acquire the collectibles he wanted to possess by any means. We've found out that that person had contact with some unsavory characters in New York City."

Riley was getting impatient with Bradshaw's game of not naming his so-called 'persons of interest' and irritated again by his not calling them 'suspects'. "Which suspect is it? Harding or Barkley?" He asked.

"Barkley is not eliminated, but I'll be having a talk with Mary Harding very soon." Bradshaw answered.

"So, you suspect Mary Harding of being the go-to person for Johncke? Anything from the other inspectors who attended our meeting?" Riley asked.

Bradshaw picked up a report from his desk. "Yes, they helped run down the Johncke angle and the Harding connection. The Yard's Art and Antique Squad spent time in Belfast investigating the usual persons of interest with no positive results." Having said that, Bradshaw grinned, remembering Riley's reference to the movie *Casablanca*. "But they did come up with Malachy Gallagher's suspected link to IRA terror in London."

"How about this Covington lady, Chief Inspector?"

"When she played on the European Women's Golf Tour she was friendly with another professional, Jennifer Lawton, who has been seen with Mary Harding. Could be a connection. And we can't rule Sarah Covington out of this."

Riley rose from his chair and reached across the desk to shake Bradshaw's hand. "I'm returning to the states tonight. I'd like the names of those in New York who have connections to Harding." Riley fixed his eyes on Bradshaw for five seconds before he squinted and said, "if the person is in New York City, I'll find the scumbag who killed my friend, Lem Shattuck."

Bradshaw handed Riley a handwritten page out of his notebook with three names and their New York City addresses.

"Good luck, Detective Riley. I'm putting a man on detail to watch Harding, starting tomorrow morning. If I get more on her link to the New York City underworld, I'll inform you."

25

The next morning, one of Bradshaw's men, Tony Jones, was assigned to a surveillance detail watching the activity of Mary Harding. Jones parked the van with no-see-in tinted windows across from her flat on Queen Victoria Street that served as a small antique gallery and living quarters. He observed the comings and goings of several persons carrying boxes and shopping bags. Jones suspected that what they carried were stolen antiques and Mary Harding was their fence, since she'd been charged with the receipt of stolen antiques once before. But that charge had been dropped for lack of evidence. *That's a good reason for another investigation,* he thought, *but today it's one of a higher priority...murder and robbery.*

On the third hour of Tony's surveillance, a person fitting the description of Harding left the apartment carrying one piece of luggage and a small package. She wore a brown tweed suit, tailored in a masculine cut. A black leather necktie was tied under the collar of her blue, button-down shirt. Her hair was pulled tightly in a bun resting on the back of her head. It confined every dark brown strand originating from her severe hairline. She drove an older model Bentley toward Westminster, and Jones followed her.

Mary Harding parked on a side street in Westminster and entered an upscale apartment without the piece of luggage, but she carried the package under one arm. Jones found a parking space a few doors down from the apartment. He waited and watched from there. It was two hours before Mary Harding left the apartment without the package, and drove off. Jones followed her to the motorway leading to Heathrow Airport. She entered the long-term air port parking lot as Jones called in a report to Chief Inspector Bradshaw to ask whether or not to arrest Harding.

Bradshaw's answer was delayed for a few seconds before he said, "okay, Tony, we don't have enough to make an arrest, but just find out where she's headed, and when she'll return. She may lead us to the New

York feathery connection. Oh, and give me the address of the flat she visited in Westminster."

Before terminating the call, Jones gave Bradshaw the street name and number of the flat. Then he drove up to a bobby near the exit from the parking lot to the ramp leading into the airport concourse. Jones flashed his Scotland Yard identification. "I say, mate, I need to park right here. I'm on a case."

The bobby directed him curbside. Jones left his car quickly, and he was in time to see Harding coming down the escalator from the parking garage. He followed her to the check-in counter of British Airways and waited until she received her boarding pass. After she started toward the gate, he bucked the line in front of several startled passengers waiting there. He showed the agent his credentials and asked where Harding was going, and when she'd return. He was told by the ticket agent that she was on her way to New York's Kennedy Airport and would return to London in two days.

TURNBERRY

26

It was a fine evening for golf. Randal Lyle, the Turnberry Security Chief who was recently retired from the Glasgow police force joined with Scott and Derrick Small on the Ailsa course. Randall was fifty-one years old, with a six-foot frame and a muscular body kept that way by jogging seven miles and doing 100 sit-ups every day.

At the 5th hole, a 530-yard, par 5 called, *Fin Me Oot*, a tee shot had to clear over 200 yards of heathery gorse before finding fairway. Scott was set to drive his ball, but stopped his swing when something caught his eye on a hill beyond. A young boy was bent over, looking at the ground. Because the youngster was in Scott's line of fire, Matt gave a holler of "Fore!" But the warning went unheeded. On Matt's second shout, the boy waved his arm to Scott in a gesture that told him to go ahead and hit. Scott deferred to local knowledge, and he asked Derrick about the kid's activity.

"Scott, the lad's working with a ferret." When this didn't clear Scott's puzzled expression, Derrick explained further. "He's after a rabbit, and just sent his ferret on the leash down a hole to catch one. He wants you to go ahead and hit your ball."

Scott was still a little confused about ferreting, but hit his drive over the boy and a good distance out on the fairway. When the others finished teeing off, Scott walked where the boy was kneeling. Just as he got there, he saw the kid pulling a yellowish-furred, weasel-like creature out of a hole in the ground. The strange animal held a rabbit in his bite by the neck. The boy made the ferret release the rabbit from its mouth, and he took his captive by the ears, dropping it in a burlap bag where it joined some others wriggling around inside. Scott introduced himself to the redheaded kid.

He shook Scott's hand with a look of embarrassment on his blushing, freckled face. "My name's Douglas McEwan. I'm sorry, sir, but I couldn't leave the rabbit hole just when your caddie hollered. I had my ferret down there and if I left him, he would've run away with the rabbit, for sure."

Scott took a closer look at the ferocious little animal. "No problem, Douglas. I was just curious about what you were up to."

"You're an American, sir?" Douglas asked.

"That's right," *There's something familiar about this boy.* He looked closely at Douglas' freckles and red hair. He pondered the connection. Then he remembered: Douglas fit the description of Hugh McNair's caddie as told by the English writer in McNair's journal. And the other even stronger coincidence was the same name, McEwan.

"I'd guess they don't ferret much in America," Douglas said. "I watched your drive go over my head. You're in fine shape. It was a powerful drive, sir. Will you be playin in the Open?"

"Yes. Will you watch it?"

"I'll be doing some ferreting on the Arran course in the mornings, then. Arran will be closed during the Open, and the crowd noise will keep the rabbits in their burrows. Ticket prices are much too dear for me, so I'll be watching it on telly at midday."

"I'll leave you some passes in the pro shop with Derrick Small," Scott said.

A smile lit up Douglas' face. "I hope you win against them all, Mr. Beckman." He ran through the brush with his ferret under one arm, and the burlap bag with its several squirming lumps slung over a shoulder.

After the boy left, Derrick caught up to Scott. "I let the McEwan lad do his ferreting on the course and started the lad caddying this year when he reached fourteen years."

***

They'd driven off the first tee at seven in the evening and were finishing at ten- thirty, just as the first stars appeared and the extended daylight of Scotland finally came to an end. Scott shot a 68 on the Ailsa course, and was pleased about that. He joined Derrick, Lyle and Matt for drinks and dinner at the Kilt and Jeans.

The hearty pub dinner featured a specialty of Scotland called *haggis,* made from the chopped-up heart, lungs and liver of a sheep. Those non-appealing ingredients were mixed with onions and oatmeal and boiled in the sheep's stomach, then served in that same organ. Scott thought the *haggis* washed down with a pint of Guinness Stout, tasted much better than its ingredients sounded.

The caddies for the Open started to stake out the pub. Matt told those gathered at the bar how Scott and he had done loops at El Camino, as kids, and how Scott's frequent fantasy when playing on the greens there was a make believe notion each putt was the one to win a Masters or British Open.

Matt looked at Scott and grinned. "Fantasy time is over, dude. Day after tomorrow, it's all for real."

27

S cott spent the next day away from practicing or playing golf. He picked up his credentials and allocation of Open passes while Matt was out on the Ailsa Course double-checking the distances from key landmarks for his yardage book.

At the Turnberry Pro-Shop, Derrick Small prepared for a buying spree by the Open crowd. He finished counting cash with those big hands of his, and put the pound notes and change in the cash register. When Scott entered, Derrick had moved to a table where stacks of wool sweaters with the Turnberry logo were waiting to be arranged by size and color.

"Douglas McEwan came here looking for an Open pass. Do you know anything about it, Scott?"

"Oh sure, I promised him some the other evening when he was ferreting for rabbits. Said I'd leave a pass here." Scott reached in his pocket and retrieved two from a stack. "There's one for his dad, too."

"His father's a plumber. "The McEwans are from Saint Andrews, where his ancestors were golf club makers in the eighteen hundreds. David McEwan moved here last year to find work."

Now Scott had a St. Andrews connection along with the McEwan name and the ferreter's resemblance to the description of the McEwan caddie in McNair's journal. But he thought the link was too weird to mention to Derrick at this time.

"Seems like a good kid, Derrick."

"Aye. He's a bright lad, but a bit outspoken at times when caddying. David McEwan will be thrilled to attend the Open with his son."

***

After Scott left the Pro Shop, he walked the grounds to have a look around. The large tented exposition and refreshment areas were in the final stages of construction. A bank was available on-site as well as a travel agency and a first-aid facility. Corporate courtesy tents were set up to house clients who would partake in complimentary champagne and catered meals. The area had the look of a circus midway or a state fair.

He passed by the practice range and recognized several of the more famous players hitting balls there. Some had competed in past British Opens, and won. Seeing these superstars sent a shiver down his spine. *I'm a long way from El Camino, and I've made it to the British Open to go up against the best players in the game, thanks to you, Sandy..*

Scott entered the locker room where Matt was hanging out with a few of the caddies. They were cleaning clubs and golf shoes, getting them ready for the official practice round the next day. Scott reached in his golf bag and removed an eight and a ten-degree driver. The ten-degree was in his allowed fourteen club allotment to be used when a high cutting drive was called for.

"Gotta get these checked out by the Royal and Ancient. Something called *COR*, Matt."

"Oh, the old *coefficient of restitution test…COR*," Matt proclaimed.

"Smart-ass caddie. Okay, Matt, brief me on it."

"They want to check your drivers for the trampoline effect." Scott looked as if he needed more detail, so Matt continued, "Say a golf ball hits a steel plate two feet thick at one hundred miles per hour and bounces back at seventy-five miles per hour. Then the trampoline effect or COR is zero-point-seventy-five."

"Like, seventy-five percent of the ball's energy springs back from the steel wall. Is that right?" Scott asked.

"You got it. If you relate that to your drivers, the R and A doesn't want to see any more than eighty-three percent of the applied energy or speed bounce off a driver's club face when it hits a golf ball at one hundred miles per hour or at any speed for that matter. In their one hundred miles per hour test, the golf ball cannot leave the club face at more than eighty-three miles per hour or the *COR* specification of zero-point-eighty-three is exceeded…making the driver illegal."

"How do you know about that, Matt?"

"I called the USGA at Golf House in New Jersey when the test first came out, and they explained it to me."

***

Later in the day, Scott returned to the locker room. Matt was still there.

"We passed both drivers at zero-point-eighty-two *COR*, Matt."

"That was a close one. Let's celebrate tonight with your last meal at the Kilt and Jeans. No players are allowed there after tonight."

"Okay, after I check to see how Chief Inspector Bradshaw's doing in his search for the feathery and the bad guys, I'll be there. But no more *haggis*."

LONDON

28

B radshaw found out who occupied the Westminster address that Tony Jones had followed Mary Harding to. He decided to make an impromptu call on Jennifer Lawton, the owner. He took the tube to Westminster and knocked on the door of the Lawton flat. Jennifer greeted him with a puzzled look until he explained who he was and the reason for his visit.

"I missed interviewing Mary Harding about a case I'm working on. I'm on a tight schedule, and I thought perhaps you might help me fill in a few pieces of the puzzle relating to the McNair feathery robbery."

"I'll try, but I know very little about it...although Mary did mention something about the cancellation of an auction where it was to be presented, and her client being extremely disappointed because of that. I've not heard about a robbery."

"There are other pieces in that consignment not as well promoted as the feathery by Covington."

"Oh, Mary didn't mention those, Chief Inspector."

"Ms. Lawton, you may still wonder why I'm interviewing you."

"Well, yes, I'm curious why."

"My preliminary investigation has shown you have a..." Bradshaw hesitated for the right word..."friendship with Mary Harding. As I mentioned, I wanted to schedule an interview with her, but she left London before I could do so."

"Yes, she left for New York City today."

Jennifer led him down a hallway through the apartment toward a sitting room. It was a grand old apartment with high ceilings and hardwood floors. Bradshaw guessed there were ten rooms connected to the hallway leading from the spacious and well-appointed white tiled foyer. It was the type of flat his wife always wanted, but well beyond the salary of a Scotland Yard chief inspector.

He followed behind the tall, attractive brunette. She moved with the confident stride of an athlete...strong, but graceful. They entered a room where a fireplace glowed warmly to cut the chill of a rain-cooled London afternoon. Above the hearth, an assortment of trophies adorned a large white marble mantle. Each trophy had the figure of a woman golfer, and a small plaque at the base with Jennifer's name inscribed along with the golfing event it commemorated.

Jennifer noticed Bradshaw moving in for a closer look at the trophies. "I don't want to sound cheeky, Chief Inspector, but the trophies on the mantle are but a few of mine. If you're interested, I can show you the more important ones later...until then, what may I do for you, sir?"

"Just a few questions." Bradshaw sat down in a brown leather chair next to Jennifer. "Do you know Sarah Covington?"

She looked at Bradshaw quizzically. "Yes, I know Sarah. We played on the European Tour together. She owns the gallery where the auction of that feathery ball was to have taken place. We were close at one time during her golfing days, but drifted apart since."

Bradshaw was silent, and his blue eyes searched Jennifer's face for more from her about Sarah Covington. He was hoping she might expand on a rumor he'd heard about the mode of Sarah's sexuality, and if there was a connection between Sarah and Mary Harding.

Jennifer caught on to the direction his questioning was headed. "Sarah is a lesbian."

"Could you amplify more on your relationship with Sarah Covington?"

"I was in love with her caddie. He left to go back to America when Sarah fired him, ostensibly, because she didn't want him in a relationship with an opposing player, *me.* "

Bradshaw paused thinking about any links to Sarah's life style. "Does Sarah Covington know Mary Harding?"

"Yes, but she hates her," Jennifer said without delay.

"Oh, why so?" Bradshaw asked.

"Their competition in the golf antique business has grown intense. Mary tried to outbid Sarah for the rare collectibles. Most times Mary couldn't compete with Sarah because she lacked the funds to do so."

"Anything else about Sarah?"

"Just...Sarah is very possessive. If she wants something or wants to rid herself of something she goes all out. I understand she wants that feathery ball, and when she didn't want her caddy around me she quickly fired him with dubious provocation. After that she stifled me with her possessiveness on tour."

Bradshaw needed a pause to gather his thoughts, and he looked around the room at the golf antiques spread throughout the room in cabinets. "So you're a collector, also, Ms. Lawton?"

"I am, though on a very small scale."

"I wonder if you could help me sort out a few more things. I'd appreciate any information before I have the opportunity to interview Ms. Harding."

"I'll try to help," Jennifer offered.

"Do you know a gentleman from Sweden...a Jaspar Johncke...an antique collector?"

"No, I've never met him, but Mary has mentioned him as a client. From what I know, he's a wealthy golf antique collector who uses Mary to acquire what he wants to own."

The chief inspector looked up from his yellow legal size notepad. His blue eyes blinked nervously before he asked, "What's your present relationship with Mary Harding?"

Jennifer gave Bradshaw a hard look. "She would like to be more than a friend, and move in with me, but I don't want that kind of relationship. It's difficult for me to break off our friendship. Mary sponsored me on tour for two years before I started winning. You see, from the time I was sixteen years old, I played competitive golf around attractive, physically strong, athletic women. They have always tried to influence my sexuality, but I've rejected that lifestyle, even though I respect it."

Bradshaw was a bit taken aback by her straight answer, but recovered enough to say, "You've been amazingly candid, and I appreciate that. Please understand solving this case involves a lot of puzzle pieces. Just plodding police work on my part."

"I understand, and I've declared my lifestyle long ago, and feel most comfortable for having done so. Jennifer smiled at Bradshaw. "I've never been in the cupboard, as the Americans say, so I don't have to come out of it. I like men, you see."

Bradshaw was amused and somehow her revelation pleased him. He laughed and said, "I believe the Americans come out of the closet, not the cupboard, Ms. Lawton."

She laughed with him at the cupboard-closet terms, and it helped to ease the emotions triggered by the question he'd asked about Mary.

"Would you like some tea, Chief Inspector? We can take it in my golf room."

"Are your other trophies there?" Bradshaw asked.

"Yes, they are, and there's more golf memorabilia in that room."

They entered a much larger room than the den. Wainscoting paneled the walls and oriental rugs covered the floors. The dark brown leather couch and chairs were well positioned to take advantage of a huge fireplace whose hearth took up most of one wall. The remaining three walls were floor-to-ceiling stained oak display cabinets.

Jennifer moved her arm by the cabinets in a gesture of totality. "These cabinets are not all filled with my trophies. Some contain a few golf antiques. I cherish each piece dearly."

Bradshaw looked through the glass of the cabinet doors at clubs, medals, art, tableware, books and balls. One cabinet was dedicated to Jennifer's trophies and another to the golf clubs and balls used when she'd won tournaments. The third cabinet included photos of her playing companions and rivals from all over the world. There were some photos of Sarah Covington with her caddie. Bradshaw was startled when he noticed that the caddie in those photographs was the same one in a picture next to an article he'd read in the *Daily News* about the British Open long shot, Scott Beckman, the owner of the feathery. He asked Jennifer about the coincidence.

"Oh, yes. That's Matt Kemp, the caddie that was fired by Sarah Covington. He's a dear, and my first love. He called me when he was in London a week ago and wanted to meet. Because I'd scheduled a discussion with Mary to sort out things on that same evening, I couldn't. However, I'm eager to see Matt after the Open when he comes through London on his way back to America."

"I see, and my best wishes go with that meeting, Ms. Lawton."

Jennifer served the tea. Bradshaw held his cup and saucer as he walked to a display cabinet filled with antique figurines. It contained bronze and marble statuettes of women performing a variety of sporting activity. The central figure in the display was immersed in a precisely aimed spotlight. His eyes fixed on the highlighted bronze of a nude woman golfer, posed at the top of her backswing. His astonishment caused his teacup to rattle in the saucer. It was the same, one-of-a-kind, bronze statuette shown in the photo given to him by Sarah Covington...the other piece stolen with the feathery from the Scott Beckman collection.

Jennifer saw his attention centered on the bronze, and got up from her seat at the tea table to join Bradshaw. "It's a beautiful piece of work, isn't it? I've been told there are no others like that bronze." She opened the glass doors of the cabinet and ran her hand over the nude body of the statuette. "It has become my favorite." .

Bradshaw recovered from his startling find enough to ask, "I say, where in the world did you acquire such an exquisite bronze, Ms. Lawton?"

Without hesitation, she answered, "Oh, Mary gave it to me on my birthday, just last week. Isn't it lovely?"

Bradshaw placed his cup and saucer down on the tea table, and the empathy he felt for Jennifer Lawton showed in his eyes when he said, "Ms. Lawton, I must take this bronze statuette from you as evidence. It was stolen, along with the feathery ball from the same collection owned by Scott Beckman, slated for auction at the Covington Gallery."

She put her hands over her face. "Oh no, not Mary!"

"Yes, I'm afraid so." He hesitated a few seconds for her to regain composure before he asked, "I have information that Mary Harding came here before she drove to the airport. She brought a package into your flat and left without it."

There were tears streaming down Jennifer's face when she said, "yes, Mary told me it contained something very valuable, and she wanted me to keep it until she returned from New York."

"Would you please bring that package to me?" Bradshaw asked.

Jennifer left the room and came back a few minutes later with a cardboard box. Bradshaw took a penknife from his pocket and slit the tape covering the two flaps. Inside he found another box made of wood. It took him a few seconds to determine how to open it by sliding the cover along the grooves on each side. When he did so, it exposed a yellowed parchment with numbers on it, dated...*St Andrews, July 8, 1849*. He lifted the record scorecard, and underneath was the feathery golf ball with *Hugh, 78* and the pennyweight *26* inscribed on it. Seeing the long-lost feathery there sent a trill cascading through Bradshaw's body.

***

Back in his office at the Yard, Bradshaw phoned Riley in New York. "We've just caught a remarkable break in the case, Detective Riley."

"Any arrest?" Riley asked, impatiently.

"None quite, but I have solid evidence. Both the feathery and statuette are in my possession."

"Wow, that is good news! How did it all happen so fast?" Riley asked.

"By chance, I stumbled on the bronze statuette while interviewing Mary Harding's friend Jennifer Lawton. It's a sad circumstance. Evidently, Mary was so desperate to win over Jennifer's affection she took the risk of giving her the bronze as a birthday gift."

"That was a risky move on Harding's part, but I guess love is an emotion that rises above caution. Where do we go from here?"

"Mary Harding will be landing at Kennedy Airport in three hours. Could you pick her up there? She may lead you to the one who murdered your friend, Shattuck."

Riley's voice on the phone became loud and clear. "I'll be waiting at Kennedy for Ms. Harding's arrival."

Bradshaw provided Riley with Harding's flight information. "I'll fax you a photo of her taken by one of my men yesterday. Tally-ho the fox, and good hunting."

TURNBERRY

29

Scott's practice round on Wednesday with Bob Bray went well. It was a happy reunion for both players and caddies. Bob's winning ways since Q-School ranked him in the top twenty-five money winners on tour, and his recent perk was a share in a Gulfstream V. Bray and two other players, who owned part of the leased aircraft, flew the Atlantic with their caddies, landing at Prestwick. Claudio Spencer was still Bob's caddie, and he apologized again to Scott about connecting him through his Uncle Anthony to Carrabba.

After the round, Scott and Matt spent two hours on the range and putting green. Scott hit a poor shot out of a bunker on the course, so he hit fifty similar ones from the practice sand until he was satisfied with the results. They were the next-to-last players to leave the range. Tiger Woods was hitting two-iron shots over a target 250 yards away while his caddie, Steve Williams, and swing coach, Hank Haney, lurked nearby.

"Tiger's going to keep his driver in the bag, and hit long irons off the tee, Scott. Good course management here."

"Okay, Matt. I know…I know. It'll be a irons for tee shots on some holes for me."

***

Matt left to join Claudio and the other caddies at the Kilt and Jeans, and Scott met Bob Bray in the dining room at the Turnberry Hotel. Scott noticed Randal Lyle there sitting alone, and he asked the security head to join them. They began a lively discussion about gambling on British Open golf.

"The R and A and the USGA do not condone wagering by players, but they haven't placed any controls on it during the Open," Randal said. "Of course, a player betting against himself would be subject to an investigation."

"The odds are tempting, Randal. Scott thought of the bet Matt had placed on him at 200 to 1 in London but didn't mention it.

"Yes they are. Wagering on golf in Scotland and throughout the UK is a legal activity." Randal added. "Millions of pounds are bet on the Open each year."

"Have there ever been any problems due to the betting?" Scott asked.

"Some minor ones, like someone in the gallery cheering when a rival to the player he has a wager on misses a putt. We take care of that quickly by ejecting the buffoon from the premises."

Bray was reading a Fleet Street tabloid and started going down the list of betting odds on players at the Open. "I'm eighteen to one...not bad." Bray continued until he came to the last name on the list. It was Scott Beckman at two hundred to one. He said, "wow, I'd take a piece of that if it was legal."

Scott glanced at his watch, and stood up from the table. "I've got to go. I'm meeting a friend at Prestwick Airport."

"Is it a woman friend or guy friend?" Bray asked.

"A lady I met in Monterey."

"Best kind, a California girl. I married one." .

Scott didn't bother telling Bray that Beth was from New York, but he shook his hand and wished him good luck tomorrow...the first day of British Open play.

30

The ramp at Prestwick Airport was crowded. Airplanes belonging to golf's finest, past and present, were parked there. They had markings symbolic of their famous owners. Scott saw a plane with a golden bear on its nose, and two others, one with a ferocious-looking tiger, and the other with a great white shark on its nose.

A set of landing lights in the distance indicated that Beth's flight was on the final approach. The sleek jet touched down gently and decelerated to make a smooth turn onto the taxiway. A man holding a strobe light in each hand guided it into a space on the ramp. The silver Boeing 737 braked to a stop, and the engines suddenly stopped screaming.

Beth Sweeney was one of the first to exit the plane. She was wearing a brown leather jacket and designer jeans. A New York Yankee baseball cap was doing its very best to control her mass of curly jet-black hair. Scott noticed the hair had grown back to the same length it had been in Monterey when he'd first toweled it dry.

When she reached him, he gathered her into his arms. Once again, after much too long those expressive eyes looked up at him when she asked, "Are you ready for tomorrow?"

"Should be, Beth, I've been practicing all week."

***

During the drive to Turnberry, Beth briefed him on the auction results at Covington Gallery and her meeting with Sarah Covington.

"Did I make enough at the auction to pay your legal fees?" Scott asked.

"More than enough." She reached in her briefcase and showed him a check for 91,000 pounds sterling. "That's about $160,000 at the current exchange rate."

"Great! How about the penalty for pulling the feathery out of the auction?"

"That's the best of it. Sarah settled for $20,000 instead of the $200,000. She just wanted enough to cover her expenses in promoting the feathery. You don't have to pay her the 20K until after the Open."

"Then it's a different Sarah than I knew from our meeting in London."

"Really?" Beth looked surprised. "Sarah was very nice to me. Took me to dinner in the Soho...showed me around London. Even drove me to the airport." A thought came into Scott's mind...*a vision of the empty slot for the McNair feathery in that display he'd seen in Sarah's golf antique collection.* "That's some turnaround. She charmed you."

"And that's not all. Sarah offered her cottage to us. It's on the sea in Portpatrick, at the tip of Scotland." Beth's smile was coquettish when she added, "I accepted on your behalf."

One of Scott's eyebrows lifted. "That might be a good place to wind down after the Open." He glanced over at her. "Can you get a few days off?"

She answered quickly, "I'm pretty sure I can."

"Let's plan on going there." Sarah's change in attitude was puzzling him. "Did Sarah mention anything about wanting to buy the McNair feathery?"

"Yes, she said to tell you she's holding firm on her offer for the feathery."

"It's not for sale if it's ever recovered."

***

It was late when they finished dinner in the Turnberry Hotel dining room. Scott walked Beth to her room. They parted after a long kiss, both wanting more. But Beth declared the lateness of the hour and Scott's need for rest before starting the first day of the British Open the next morning.

Shortly after Scott entered his room, the phone rang. It was Chief Inspector Bradshaw.

"Hope I didn't catch you too late. First off, I'd like to wish you all the best in the Open tomorrow."

"Thanks. I'm looking forward to playing. I feel fortunate to be here, and I think I'm ready. How's the case going?"

"Very well. We've located the persons who had your feathery and bronze statuette in their possession."

Scott sighed with relief. "Where are they? Where did you find them?"

"I've confiscated the items and logged them in as evidence. I located both the statue and the feathery during an interview with a..." he paused for the correct term to describe Mary Harding's relationship with Jennifer Lawton, and settled on..."friend of the suspect."

"Friend?" Scott asks.

"Yes, a very lovely lady who's a professional golfer. In fact, Matt Kemp, your own caddie had a relationship with her when he caddied on the European women's tour for none other than Sarah Covington."

Scott thought, *That must be part of the long story Matt mentioned in Santa Barbara. He'll finish telling me about it when he's ready.* "What's next Chief Inspector?

"We need to know who's responsible for the shootings in New York and Heathrow. And we're working hard on that as we speak."

"Wow, you've got the feathery. How soon will this all be over?"

"Very soon. Possibly before you finish play, we may have the suspects, as you Americans call them, in custody." The chief inspector chuckled out loud. "Just concentrate on your game, Scott, and I'll update you later."

When Scott put down the phone, his mind switched from the recovered antiques to the way he would play the first, second and third holes of Turnberry's Ailsa course. Sleep came to him when his mind reached a vision of the third fairway.

NEW YORK CITY

31

D etective Riley arrived at Kennedy just as British Airways Flight 1104 landed. He double-checked the photo of Mary Harding and then showed it to the immigration agents who'd clear the flight. Riley's eyes were glued on the passengers as they streamed through the customs checkpoint.

He was getting anxious after fifty passengers or so showed their passports and moved on toward customs. Finally, there she was among the stragglers. She wore a masculine-cut tweed suit, and her brown hair was pulled straight back in a bun just as it was in the photograph. When Mary reached the agent and started to present her passport, Riley stepped forward.

"Are you Mary Harding?" Riley asked.

The sight of his NYPD detective's badge bewildered her. "Why yes, I'm she...What's the meaning of this?"

"You're under arrest for an alleged complicity dealing with armed robbery and murder. Anything you say now may be held against you in a court of law."

Next came the handcuffs, and a matron from the department walked up to escort Mary to an unmarked car waiting curbside outside the terminal. Riley joined Harding in the backseat, and the policewoman got in beside the driver. Harding was visibly shaken. Riley thought the 'good cop' approach might work best.

"Mary, we have solid evidence implicating you in the robbery of an antique feathery golf ball and a bronze statuette. It's over Mary. Scotland Yard has both items in their possession as evidence."

"Oh, my God...Jennifer! She's not involved in this."

"I know that, Mary." He made eye contact with her before he continued. "I don't think you wanted this heist to go down with getting a man killed and another wounded. Am I right?"

She nodded rapidly. "I had no idea they'd do that."

Riley took advantage of the moment. "If you cooperate with us in apprehending the shooters, I'll do everything I can to make sure it's considered at your trial. This is very personal to me because the guard killed here in New York was a friend of mine."

Harding looked over at Riley. "Those hopped up fools. Now they've threatened me and want payment of the other half of the agreement. I'm supposed to meet with them at four this afternoon."

Riley's question was sudden and sharp. "Will you wear a wire at that meeting, Mary?"

Harding waited only a few seconds before she said, "yes, I'll do that."

***

At four o'clock in the afternoon, Riley was sitting in a surveillance van with two FBI agents. They watched Harding enter a brownstone apartment building in Lower Manhattan. She tapped the microphone on her chest to test the wire. The lines on a display jumped simultaneously, and a couple of thuds came from two audio speakers in the van. The FBI technician gave Riley a thumbs-up signal indicating the wire was in place and working fine.

When Mary entered the apartment the technicians heard background noise and the shuffling of chairs on the electronic surveillance equipment. Following that, harsh preliminary greetings were punctuated with swear words. Their hospitality consisted of offering Mary a line of cocaine, which she denied.

One voice said, "the fucking guys we hired in England to do the thing at Heathrow want more dough from your Swede friend. They've gotta hide out in Spain because Scotland Yard is closing in on their ass."

"The Swede, Johncke, is dead," Mary said.

The same voice as before asked, "somebody fucking whack him?"

"No, heart attack," Mary answered.

"Shit! Anyway, you got the fifty grand in that briefcase?"

"Yes."

"Let's have it."

"I have a question first," Mary said.

"No fucking questions," came the reply by the same raspy voice.

Anyway, Mary asked the question Detective Riley wanted her to.

"Why did you shoot the guard at the Covington Gallery here in New York?"

"I shot the asshole because he pulled his fucking gun on me."

They'd heard enough. Detective Riley followed behind an NYPD officer whose battering ram dislodged the apartment door from its hinges. Riley's gun was drawn as he rushed into the room with four uniformed cops. They caught the three men by surprise, and they all dropped down on the floor as ordered, which shook the glass top on the table lined with cocaine.

"Mary, which one of these coke heads killed Lem Shattuck?" Riley asked.

She pointed at the raspy voiced one who'd admitted to it.

Riley held off one of the cops heading toward Shattuck's killer. "I'll put the cuffs on this guy."

The FBI technician manning the electronic surveillance gear in the van heard a shrill scream come over the speakers. It made the video lines on his monitor display jump around like pulsating spaghetti.

TURNBERRY

32

Scott's tee time for the first day of the Open was 9:18 in the morning. He ate a large breakfast to hold off any sugar-low that might occur while playing through his normal lunchtime. He washed down three eggs over easy, fried potatoes, sausages and fried green tomatoes along with a rack of toast with a large glass of orange juice. He left the hotel at seven and walked down the long stairway leading from the hotel toward the locker room. Lines were already forming at the main gate, and masses of spectators had started funneling in. It was their yearly pilgrimage to the British Open…a Mecca-like journey for golf fans from all over the world. A large gallery was expected today, Thursday, the first day. The crowds would increase until peaking on Sunday, the final day.

Scott entered the locker room, and the attendant there greeted him with encouraging words. "It's a fresh morning, sir, and the weather should stay fine for play."

Matt was sitting on a bench with Scott's golf bag standing next to him. All clubs had been cleaned and he'd dotted a dozen new balls in a pattern that would distinguish them as Scott's if the ownership of a ball in play should be questioned. He placed the balls in the proper pockets of the bag along with four golf gloves, two bananas and an energy bar.

Scott sat on the bench and started to put on his golf shoes. He said, "are we ready for this, Matt?"

"Piece of cake, master. We own a betting slip on you at two hundred to one."

They left for the practice range where some of the players were talking about the odds placed on them. The favorite was at six to one, while the other betting odds ranged upward to the long shot, Scott Beckman. A few players were tempted by the high odds beside their names, and sent their caddies to the betting shops in town to lay down a wager on themselves.

Scott started practice by hitting a gap-wedge aimed at a target flag 65 yards away. He then worked his way through the irons and woods until it was time for the driver.

Bob Bray arrived at the range just as Scott was about to leave for the putting green. They wished each other the best. Bray gave Scott a tip about the pace of play. "In a major tournament where the stakes are highest, some playing partners will try to slow you down or speed you up," Bray advised. "Play at your own pace to maintain good tempo."

After ten minutes on the putting green, Scott looked up to see Sarah Covington quietly watching him from the other side of the ropes. He handed Matt his putter and walked over to her. She was dressed in a well-fitted white linen suit with a light blue blouse with a matching scarf hung loosely around its collar.

"Hello, Sarah. Thanks for reducing the penalty for my taking the feathery out of the auction."

"Oh, Beth was more charming than you." She smiled. "Beth reached my soft spot. I'm scheduled to attend several antique golf meetings today. The first one is at nine...so I must run. Just wanted to say hello and wish you good play."

"Are you staying in Portpatrick?" Scott asked.

"Yes, I'm leaving early this evening to escape the Open traffic. Are you and Beth planning to stay at my cottage after the Open?"

"I'm looking forward to it. And thanks for that."

"Good, I'm off now. Good luck today." She started walking away, then stopped abruptly, turning back toward Scott. "By the way, I heard a rumor that your feathery has been recovered." Her eyes narrowed. "I'd still like to buy it."

That vision of the four-golf ball display he'd seen in her gallery with the empty slot waiting for the McNair feathery came to Scott again. "Sorry, it's still not for sale, Sarah."

She glared at him before she spun around and hurried away.

Scott watched her until she merged into the crowded midway, and he walked slowly back to the heart of the practice green where Matt gathered several Titleists for Scott to putt toward a hole 21 feet away.

As Matt handed him his putter he said, "that was Sarah Covington, right? Watch your back, Scott."

Scott looked up at Matt from the putt he was about to strike and said, "get over it, Matt."

Before Matt could respond, they were called to the first tee.

***

It was handshakes all around between playing partners and officials. The others in Scott's threesome were an Australian and a Swede. They waited a few minutes for the group in front to clear the first fairway and reach the green. The gallery at the first tee was larger than Scott expected, and he thought the fame of his playing partners was responsible for that. He recognized the young ferreter, Douglas McEwan, standing beside a tall man resembling his son, only with fewer freckles and a lighter shade of red hair. Scott walked over to the McEwans and shook their hands. Douglas introduced Scott to his father.

Douglas' grin was wide. "I told my da you're a better player than the betting shop odds show you to be. You can win against them all, sir."

The last part of Douglas' statement was said in a louder voice than he realized. Those on the tee and in the crowd laughed as the freckles on Douglas' face disappeared in a sea of red. Scott tousled his curly head of hair and walked back to the tee.

Before they hit their first drives to start their quest for the Claret Jug trophy, the announcer introduced the players to the gallery. A resumé of their past successes came with that announcement. The first two players hit drives over a group of bunkers, landing on the left edge of the fairway about 275 yards away. They were safe drives and positioned well.

The announcer introduced Scott next. The loudspeaker reverberated with a Scottish lilt. "Next on the tee, Scott Beckman from San Diego, California, in the United States of America." There was a ripple of applause from the gallery. Douglas McEwan extended his clapping long after the others ceased. He received a severe look from a marshal holding up a *QUIET PLEASE* sign.

Matt whispered to Scott, "at least you have one enthusiastic fan in the gallery." He handed Scott his two iron.

The first hole was not difficult. Scott expected a birdie there to duplicate the many he had during his practice on this Ailsa Course. His drive flew over the farthest bunker on the right side, 260 yards out. A slight draw after the ball passed the last bunker made it roll to a stop 280 yards from the tee, in perfect position for an eight iron to the green.

Scott walked by the McEwans on his way off the tee and heard Douglas say, "I told you he could hit it, da."

Scott got the birdie he wanted on the first hole. On the way to the second tee he looked out at the Ailsa Craig, and the black granite rock was clearly dominant across the dark blue waters of the Firth of Clyde. A large flock of gannets were diving for fish out on Turnberry Bay. Scott remembered the local tenet, "If ye can't see the Ailsa Craig it's rainin' and if ye can, it's *aboot* to rain." He could see it clearly today, and would make the best of that, but the local knowledge assured that this San Diego-type weather was *aboot* to change.

***

Scott Beckman completed the first day of the British Open at 66, five under par, and in first place. This unexpected revelation brought a buzz of wondrous excitement throughout Turnberry, and it was passed on to the millions watching on television. Scott's score brought him under scrutiny by the world's golf writers, and he spent an hour in the media tent answering their questions. They wanted background on the player who led the Open even though he was ranked 182nd on the PGA earned money list. Their writings and commentary would speculate whether or not this first day *rabbit's* outstanding play would continue.

Scott and Matt spent an hour on the practice range. After they finished, Matt left for the Kilt and Jeans and Scott for the hotel...neither of them knowing the consternation a betting shop mogul, Ian Barkley, had over the chance Scott's good play would continue throughout the tournament.

LONDON

33

Ian Barkley was a frustrated gambling czar as he stared at the BBC television channel and very loudly said, "Malachy, come." His voice was a clap of thunder crashing among the low hum of cooling fans whirring inside the mass of electronic surveillance devices that monitored his gambling empire. The intercom system sent his command throughout the thirty-room mansion in pursuit of his indentured man-servant.

Barkley sat at the master control panel in his operations center, stark naked as usual. He was watching a lettered announcement running across the bottom of a big screen plasma television set: **OPEN FIRST ROUND LEADER IS AN AMERICAN LONG SHOT, SCOTT BECKMAN. KUNIAKI YAMAZAKI OF JAPAN IS IN SECOND PLACE WITH SCOTLAND'S MacGREGOR TIED WITH THREE OTHERS FOR THIRD.**

Barkley's two stubby index fingers flew about the keyboard to type an inquiry into his computer. The master monitor soon filled with the information he asked for. His eyes narrowed to slits as he read the British Open wagering summary from his network of 150 betting shops.

When Malachy Gallagher entered the room, Barkley indicated the information on the computer display. "We may have a problem at the Open. Before it started we placed odds of two hundred to one on a golfer who leads the tournament by a near-record score of sixty-six on the first day." Barkley sent a sour look Malachy's way. "Our odds-makers were wrong, and I could lose millions."

To strengthen his point, Barkley clicked on his mouse to gain more data from his gambling kingdom. The computer display listed wagers placed on Scott Beckman before play started. The field on the screen showed the type of bet, the amount and the betting shop where they'd been placed. Many punters had gone for the high odds at the start on a whim. This was evident by the 2460 bets at five pounds each showing up on the data summoned by Barkley. The bet made at Barkley's Trafalgar

Shop in London was the largest single bet shown in these data, at 500 pounds.

"With three days left, thousands will go for him even at our lowered odds," Barkley said, as he continued to view his projected losses. "This computer is telling me I could take a hit of over eight million pounds if this Beckman chap is still around on Sunday."

Malachy made a comment, though it was rare he would interrupt his master's tirades. But he hoped to hold off a mission like the others of fixing jockeys and football players and drugging horses. He said, "It's only the first day. There are three more to go."

Barkley turned slowly around in his swivel chair to face Malachy. "I know, but we must be ready in case this Beckman bloke isn't a flash in the pan." He gave Malachy a hard look and an order after he'd thought out a plan. "If Beckman is still in a winning position when Friday's play is complete, I want you and your friends to take his caddie for a boat ride. You are to inform the others to meet you in Turnberry tomorrow morning, ready to act on Friday evening, if necessary."

"Why not kidnap Beckman, sir?" Malachy blurted.

Barkley sent a stern look Malachy's way before he hissed his answer between closed lips. "Because, Mr. Pub Bomber, the security for players at Turnberry is much tighter than for caddies."

TURNBERRY

34

It was seven in the morning on Friday, the second day of the Open, the day in a golf tournament known as "moving day" by the players, when they were either cut or they moved on to the finishing rounds. The atmosphere on the driving range had changed to reflect the tension brought on by that pivotal point. Once again, the weather was more like California than Scotland.

Scott took advantage of the rare tranquil air to make some birdies and an outstanding eagle on number 17, Lang Whang, finishing with an awesome 65. The virtually unknown American was the second-day leader of the British Open with an impressive total of 131. A stiff wind started to blow in from the Firth of Clyde to plague others who were still out on the course trying to climb up the leader board.

Media frenzy held Scott in the press tent for a over an hour. He was interviewed live on television They wanted to know where he'd been hiding a golf game that led the British Open after two days of play. One of the anchors was an All American college player and past PGA touring pro from California. When Scott mentioned that Sandy McNair was his mentor, he was all over the story about Scott's early background. The TV commentator knew Sandy and had taken lessons from him when he was on tour.

When Scott finally got to the practice range, Matt's exuberance over Scott's lead was apparent, and a little distracting to his player's concentration. Scott released his caddie from the range early, and Matt promptly made a beeline for the Kilt and Jeans. He would be there to watch the other players finish on television as they fought the strong wind. And The Kilt and Jeans would be the right place for him to celebrate if Scott still held on to the lead.

***

After practice, Scott visited the Expo tents and bought two cashmere sweaters. The soft wool would retain body warmth, even when wet, and ward off the chill of the Linksland storm in the forecast. He was drawn to a booth there filled with golf antiques. The owner came over as he was peering into a glass case displaying feathery golf balls.

"You're Scott Beckman. I recognized you from the telly. Congratulations on your play. I'm John Hollbrooke."

Scott shook his outstretched hand and wondered if all men involved with antiques sported goatees and ponytails like Gamby and Hollbrooke. "Thanks, I'm admiring your collection of feathery balls."

"Quite, Gourlay, Robertson and McNair from Saint Andrews made these in the mid-eighteen hundreds." Hollbrooke took a key from his pocket to unlock and open the case. He put on white silk gloves and handed a pair to Scott saying, "I'll fetch a McNair ball for you."

Scott ran his fingers over the leather and squeezed against the surprising hardness of the ball. He thought of another McNair feathery marked with the record number 78. Mr. Hollbrooke interrupted his muse.

"According to Sarah Covington, you own a ball much more valuable than the one in your hand."

Scott handed the feathery back to Hollbrooke and took off the gloves "You know Sarah?"

"Oh, yes. Everyone in this business knows her. She was here today and told me about your stolen feathery. Dastardly buggers."

Scott thought, *Evidently Sarah didn't tell Hollbrooke there was a rumor the feathery was recovered. Possible competition from him.*

Hollbrooke waved at someone in the crowd walking the Expo aisle. It was the McEwans.

Douglas cried out, "Beat them all tomorrow, Mr. Beckman." Douglas started to head toward them until he was restrained by his father, who might have been embarrassed by his son's outburst. They waved again and were lost in the crowd.

"I see you know the McEwans, Mr. Beckman."

"Yes, I first met the boy when he was ferreting on the course."

"Did you know their ancestors were well-known craftsmen of golf clubs in Saint Andrews during the eighteen hundreds?"

"Derrick Small mentioned that to me."

"I've tried to buy several antique McEwan drivers and spoons passed down to David, but he won't sell. One of the drivers is worth a fortune, and I believe they could use the money."

"Family tradition can be strong, Mr. Hollbrooke. Thanks for giving me a chance to touch a feathery again."

"My pleasure, sir, and if yours is recovered, I'd like to buy it. Keep me in mind."

"Thanks Mr. Hollbrooke, but it won't be for sale."

LONDON

35

Malachy Gallagher approached the ticket window at Houston Station in London. A young woman ticket-seller peered out from behind her cage at the short man with scars over his eyebrows and both ears distorted into a strange shape. He held a duffel bag in one fist. It looked like the same bag her boyfriend took to the gym when he worked out. Malachy asked for a first class ticket on the night train to Glasgow. His deep voice carried an accent the ticket agent readily recognized as Irish. She tried to guess the man's profession as she handed him a ticket and his change and chanced a two-word inquiry to validate her speculation. "Prize Fighter?" she asked.

His answer amounted to a scowl in her direction. He spun around and hurried away from the ticket window as the clerk's middle finger popped up under her cage. Her, "up yours, mate," didn't reach the Irishman as he quickly walked away toward the train platform.

The late train to Scotland had few passengers. He'd chosen train travel instead of air to avoid the airport search and X-ray. Malachy was the only passenger occupying a six-person compartment, and he hoped it would stay that way.

The train moved slowly over the rails as it started out of the station. He stood up to draw the shade on his compartment's sliding door and reached for the duffel bag on the luggage rack above. He opened it, took out a bottle of Jameson Irish Whiskey and placed it on the shelf by the window. The other items tucked into the same bag were a 38 special pistol, some rope and a roll of duct tape. He checked the contents of a small box. Inside it lying on white cotton was a scalpel.

He zipped up the duffel bag and settled back in his seat. Malachy stared at the Jameson and looked out the compartment window at the night. As the train's speed increased, the click-clack of the car's wheels as they passed over cross-ties soon became one continuous tone. Raindrops streaked as they hit the window glass making the buildings along side the track a dark, wet blur.

Those sounds and the view out of the window bought him back to another rainy night when he was nineteen years old on a train heading toward London from Belfast. He was on a mission then even more deadly than this one. Northern Ireland was split between Catholic and Protestant factions, and Belfast was the center of that combat. After the Orange killed his father, it was rock-throwing and street fights at first…then at seventeen he joined the IRA for a more organized fight for the cause. He was ordered to retaliate against the English, and his assignment was to place bombs in London pubs.

The bottle of whiskey was still unopened as the Glasgow express continued on through the dank English countryside. He remembered how he'd carried out the orders of IRA leaders and was chilled by the ruthlessness of those acts. The whiskey made it easier then, but he'd quit the drink two years ago hoping abstinence would offer absolution for his past terrorism. It didn't help, and the same violent acts continued in different ways.

His isolation in the darkened compartment accommodated a reflection on the situation he was now in: *The reason Barkley has given me a safe house and employment is because he knows of my IRA history. And the bastard continues to use this threat of exposure to benefit his gambling empire by forcing me to be part of a team fixing the results of sporting events. I wish I could walk away from all this, but Barkley's arm is long.*

"When will it stop?" It was as if he was asking those empty seats for an answer and forgiveness. His eyes focused on the Jameson again, and he came close to breaking his vow to quit the drink. His thoughts went to the purpose of this trip to Scotland and he spoke out loud again. "Barkley never wants to lose."

He pulled a newspaper clipping out of his leather jacket pocket. It was cut out from the *London Evening News,* sports section, and the headline read: YANK LONG SHOT HAS OPEN LEAD. There was a large photo of Scott Beckman with his caddie, Matt Kemp. Malachy was more interested in Kemp's features than Beckman's.

He stared at the photo for a moment before putting it back in his pocket. His next muse was an attempt to offer rationalization for what he'd been ordered to do. *For fuck sake, did this spoiled American country club golfer and his caddie with their wealthy, doting fathers have to go through what I did as a lad after my old man gave his life for the IRA cause?*

TURNBERRY

36

Matt sat at the bar of the Kilt and Jeans pub savoring his first beer. His eyes were focused on the television screen above. Play was concluding and it was apparent none of the other players were going to bump Scott from the lead. When the BBC confirmed the second day leader was Beckman, Matt's happy screech rung throughout the pub. It signaled his fellow caddies to approach him with high fives, fist-to-fist punches and handshakes. It was party time, and Matt's party. But first, he'd phone Scott who was paged by a member of the Turnberry Hotel staff.

"Matt, buddy, we've come a long way from doing loops at El Camino." Scott said. "We're leading the British Open. Can you believe it? Come on over to the hotel."

"Naw, why break tradition? It might be bad luck. I'll hang out here with the rest of the Sherpas and groupies. I'll meet you in the morning in the locker room. We need to be ready for the rain and wind that's on its way over from Ireland."

"Okay, See you then."

Matt put the phone on the cradle and left the booth. He noticed an attractive girl leaning against the wall.

"Sorry I was so long in there," Matt spoke to her, assuming she was waiting to use the phone.

"Oh, that's quite all right," she said. "I'm not in a hurry. Are you here for the Open golf?"

Her voice sounded deep and sexy with its Irish lilt. Matt was taken in by it and he said, "yes, I'm a caddie and my player leads it."

"Congratulations. May I come by later to help you celebrate...ah?" She hesitated waiting for his name.

"Name's Matt Kemp, and I'll be sitting at the bar."

She put her hand in his. "I'm Sandra. I'll look you up there after I make my call."

Her ample breasts brushed his shoulder as she entered the phone booth. The booth's dome light came on, activated by the switch as its glass door closed behind her. When Matt saw the silhouette of Sandra's body, a stronger urge to have her join him came in a hormonal rush.

Five minutes later, Sandra slipped onto the stool next to him. She ordered a beer and said, "tell me about the Open, Matt."

After some talk and some close dancing, Matt decided to accept her invitation to leave the Kilt and Jeans for another bar in the village of Maidens, nearby. A late-arriving caddie friend approached them to offer his congratulations. Matt introduced the caddie to Sandra and then turned aside to give his friend a run-down on Scott's round. He missed the quick transfer of two pills from Sandra's hand into the white foam of Matt's beer. The pills sank down through the froth, and before they reached the bottom of the pint, the dosage had melded with the golden brew.

Matt finished talking to his friend, and the caddie left the bar to join some others at a table. After twenty minutes and a few more swallows to finish the pint, he was ready to leave with Sandra. When he got up from his stool, a spell of queasiness hit him and he thought, *How can I feel this way after only a couple of beers?*

Sandra answered that thought. "You're probably tired after today's excitement and need some fresh air," she urged, "Come, let's go."

When they reached the parking lot, Matt started to lose feeling in his legs. His last semiconscious thought was, *is this woman strong enough to hold me up?*

Two pairs of stronger arms relieved Sandra of her burden. Behind them lurked a shorter man with cauliflower ears and scars above both his eyebrows. The big ones threw Matt into the back seat and joined him on each side. Malachy took the wheel of the Renault with Sandra seated beside him. The car squealed rubber leaving the parking lot as Matt slipped down into a dark void of nothingness.

LARNE, NORTHERN IRELAND

37

When Matt awoke, he heard the sound and motion of a boat charging through rough waters. He was blindfolded with duct tape. Above the noise made by the boat's engines he could hear more than one muffled male voice. His first mottled thoughts came with an attempt to rationalize the carelessness that'd got him here. *My caution was clouded by the excitement of Scott having the lead.*

The boat continued to smack the waves, and the smell of diesel oil combined with its motion to make him nauseous. When his body numbness started to wear off he felt a tingling sensation in his left ear. He couldn't reach up to check out the bothersome sensation because his hands were tied to the bunk. He wondered, *Is my pierced earlobe infected?* Then he thought it silly to worry about such a small irritation when he'd been drugged and kidnapped…and most likely facing other harm.

After what seemed like hours, the boat started to slow. The engine quieted to idle, and he could hear voices with Irish accents shouting commands during the docking. Matt's heartbeat raced and the place where his left earlobe should be was throbbing at the same fast rate. He sensed a strong grip on each arm pulling him off the bunk and leading him down a ramp into a car.

Malachy Gallagher quietly left the boat, unnoticed, while the others finished the docking and the off-loading of their abducted passenger. In his right fist he carried the duffel bag containing the 38-pistol, duct tape, bottle of Jameson whiskey and the box with a blood stained scalpel inside. When he reached the end of the dock, out of sight from those on the boat, Malachy tossed the duffel bag far out into the water of the harbor with a strong over-hand throw. After he heard it splash, he said in a whisper, "I'm done with Barkley and this business. For fuck sake, I haven't even visited or called my mum in four years." He quickly walked two blocks, entered a phone booth, called his mother and, after talking to her, hailed the taxi that would take him to Belfast.

***

The ride for Matt was only about ten minutes until the same arm constraints walked him up some stairs. With his blindfold still in place, he guessed he was entering a building when he heard a door open and close.

They took off his blindfold in one quick motion that brought a few eyebrow hairs with the duct tape. The strong-armed men on each side of him were wearing ski masks. They sat him down on the wide boards of a wooden floor whose red paint was chipped and faded. Matt looked around a room void of any furnishings. His back rested against a black wall that had chunks of white where the plaster was missing. A shade was pulled down to cover the only window, and one bare bulb hung by its electrical cord from the ceiling to serve as the only dim lighting in the room. He looked up at his ski-masked captors. They were both large, and the larger of the two spoke first.

"Just relax, caddie. We're going to hold you here for a couple of days until the Open is over. Don't try to get away. It won't be looked on kindly." He waved an automatic weapon...*maybe an AK-47*, Matt thought.

The smaller, but still big, guy spoke, "I'm going to free your hands now." With that announcement he slipped a knife out from the leather sheath hanging on his belt. He made two swift cuts on the material that bound Matt's wrists together. "There now...you may want to rub those wrists to get the circulation back." His brogue was just as Irish as the bigger one's.

Instead of rubbing his wrists, Matt's left hand went quickly up to his left ear. He felt a bandage there, but couldn't detect an ear lobe or a gold ring. "What the hell have you guys done to my ear?"

The biggest answered, "Minor surgery, lad."

"Was that fucking necessary?" Matt asked.

The guy who'd used his knife to cut Matt's wrist constraints growled an answer. "Orders from headquarters."

"Jeez, did you use that knife?" Matt pointed to the sheath on not-so-big's belt and glared up at him. "How about infection?" he asked in a pissed-off tone.

"Don't worry," the knife wielder said. "It was done with a clean scalpel and disinfected after. I'll change the bandage and clean it up a bit later."

The biggest one left the room first, and the other, who'd declared the minor surgery sanitary, reached the doorway and stopped there. He said, "hang in, Matt; It'll be over soon. I'll be back with some food and drink."

Matt dozed off, and when he woke up he looked around the room for a few seconds trying to recall where he was and what had happened. After he established it was not all a bad dream, but a real horror, he touched the spot where his earlobe used to be. It was sore and still throbbing. He could hear talk with music playing in the background, and those sounds were coming from the next room. Matt recognized an old song by The Clancy Brothers.

After a while, the smallest of the biggest kidnappers entered the room carrying a roast beef sandwich on soda bread and a soft drink. He set them down beside Matt and said, "I'll be back later to work on that ear."

He returned in a half hour with a bottle of alcohol, some Q-tips and a Band-Aid. As he changed the dressing on the ear he started whispering into it, "Don't speak to me until I tell you to, and only in a whisper then. I'm under cover here for Scotland Yard. I've been working as a mole on a case dealing with gaming fixes on horse races, and was not aware of the plan for your abduction until after you were snatched. So I couldn't stop it. These guys are bad-asses so we must be careful. Okay, speak to me quietly."

"This sucks," Matt whispered.

"I know, but why not wait it out? They're going to release you unharmed when Beckman withdraws from the Open."

"What happens if Scott doesn't withdraw?"

The Mole paused. He didn't want to tell Matt about their back-up plan of more ear surgery. Instead he asked, "Why can't you wait it out?"

"No good, my player has a chance to win the British Open, and he needs me there to help him do it! He just can't withdraw after two days of leading the tournament." Matt looked up at the Mole, appealing for his help. "Can't you get me out of here before it's too late?"

The Mole didn't answer Matt's question for what seemed like a long time. He finished cleaning and bandaging the ear before he whispered, "I'll give it a try. It's complicated because I'm working on getting evidence for other gambling fixes, and I don't want my cover blown. He paused into more thought before he whispered, "I might be able to pull off your release, since the others are caught up looking for the guy who organized snatching you. He defected after the boat docked, and he might be turning on the head guy, Barkley, who we're trying to get enough on to convict."

PRESTWICK

38

"Who do ya like in the Open, Joel?"

It was five in the morning after Matt's abduction, and Joel Pringle was loading the last of his packages into a white van with a blue lightening bolt zigzagging through the words: BLUE STREAK DELIVERY. The Blue Streak dispatcher asked the question.

"I'm sticking with our Scot, Allan MacGregor. He's in fourth place, overdue to win a major, and at fifty to one going in, it's a good bet."

"How about the Japanese player and that Yank, Beckman, who's leading the thing?" The dispatcher asked.

"No way. Our weather today is going to blow those two out of the tournament, Joel said."

Joel had wagered ten pounds on MacGregor at the Barkley Betting Shop in Glasgow. MacGregor's proven ability in bad weather bolstered his hope for a win to reap a payoff of 500 pounds.

The dispatcher handed him the load manifest. Joel skimmed over it, noting only a few parcels would be delivered enroute from Prestwick. Packages for the Turnberry Hotel made up the majority of his load. Included were golf products for the tented Expo area and expedited deliveries for hotel guests who'd forgotten medication, contact lenses, or the like.

He left the loading dock and drove south toward his first delivery in Ayr. Clouds hung low to mask the attempt of a rising sun to lighten up the lead-gray sky, and once beyond Ayr, sprinkles of rain began. Joel switched the windshield wipers on slow and continued driving toward darker skies.

As he drove south, Joel thought about the golfers who would play Turnberry that day. They would be facing rain and strong winds after being spoiled by two days of calm, and it would be a true test of their skills. Most all of Scotland would be watching to see how the foreign golfers handled the elements that were so much a part of golf as it was played in their country.

When the van entered the village of Maidens, Joel switched the wiper blades to high speed. Frequent bursts of rain slammed at the right side of his van as strong gusts blew in from the Firth of Clyde. The Ailsa Craig island was well hidden in the clouds.

The Blue Streak van pulled up to the guard shack at Turnberry's entrance gate. It was an hour before the first tee time. The crowd was light, but six security guards were on duty there. Joel thought this strange until he was told there'd been a bomb threat, and Security would be inspecting each package in his delivery lot. Joel unloaded his van and received a signature receipt from Turnberry Security Chief, Randal Lyle, who assured him the parcels would be delivered after the inspection.

The large drop of packages at Turnberry would allow Joel to finish his route an hour earlier and to get on the road to Glasgow. Soon, he would be cheering MacGregor on inside a warm, dry pub, watching the BBC television broadcast of the Open.

Lyle directed the guards to begin their inspection of the Blue Streak deliveries. Not long afterwards, he was called over to a bench where a small box had been opened by one of his men. The man's normal red flush had drained. His face was pale and his bulging eyes were fixed on the box he'd just opened. Lyle looked down at its contents.

Resting on top of some red-stained cotton was a gold earring hooked into a bit of flesh that resembled an earlobe. Both men stood there gazing down at the bloody contents of the package. That alone was alarming, but what really startled them were the words on a note inside the box.

The security head, Lyle, asked, "To whom is this package addressed?"

The guard expelled a gasp of air along with his answer. "The golfer, Scott Beckman, sir."

"Go find Mr. Beckman right away and bring him to my office," Lyle ordered.

39

The tournament leader's tee time was 12:06, and Scott planned to arrive in the locker room at nine that morning. He looked out through the rain streaks on his hotel room window as a strong gust turned the leaves on an oak tree over to expose their lighter shade of green. He phoned Matt's room at the Kilt and Jeans but didn't get an answer. Perhaps Matt was at breakfast or already at the course, he thought, knowing his caddie would be aware of weather reports and prepare his bag for any adverse conditions.

Scott took both new cashmere sweaters from a drawer and put the beige one on over a turtleneck. He pulled a windbreaker over both. The other sweater went in his duffel for later transfer to his golf bag if required. And with wind-chilling rain a factor he thought it could be a two-cashmere day.

Matt was not at the practice range when Scott arrived there, and he asked some of the caddies if they'd seen him. They told him that Matt hadn't made it to breakfast at the Kilt and Jeans.

A group of sports writers approached Scott, clamoring for a new spin on the American who led the Open, and he talked to them for ten minutes while keeping an eye out for his caddie, but Matt didn't show. He headed for the locker room to get his golf bag, and on the way there, he stopped at the putting green to wish Bob Bray good luck. Even though there were still more than two hours before his tee time, Scott was becoming more worried about Matt's absence. Claudio asked Scott how Matt had fared after last night's celebration.

"He's not here, and I'm wondering why."

Claudio stopped rolling golf balls back from the cup to Bob Bray and looked up at Scott. "I saw him leave the Kilt and Jeans with a lovely redhead last night. He probably overslept and he'll be here soon."

Scott left the putting green, hurried to the locker room phone and called the Kilt and Jeans desk, trying to find out if anyone there knew of Matt's whereabouts. No one at the Inn could locate him. After a chambermaid checked Matt's room, she reported that Matt's bed didn't look like it had been slept in. Scott's concern heightened. Just as he hung up the phone, the locker room attendant rushed toward him with a message. He told Scott there was a gate guard with a golf cart outside waiting to take him to Randal Lyle's office.

Scott got into the golf cart marked SECURITY and was driven toward the hotel. He guessed it was about Matt and tried to dampen his worst fears. As they sped up the hill his mind raced through all categories of accidents or illnesses that could've occurred to make his friend go missing. He struggled to maintain control as he entered the security office.

Randal Lyle was sitting behind his desk, and two local police were standing in front of Randal staring down at a box on his desk. Randal was wearing gloves to eliminate his own prints "This just arrived and it's addressed to you. It was sent from Portpatrick overnight by Blue Streak Delivery." Randal's expression made Scott brace himself for bad news as Randal slowly opened the box.

Scott stared down at the gold earring looped through a piece of flesh resting on a wad of cotton dotted with blood. He saw shocking words written on notepaper there: WITHDRAW, followed by, OR THE NEXT PACKAGE WILL CONTAIN THE REST OF YOUR CADDIE'S EAR.

Scott put both hands to his face. "Oh, no," he said, "not Matt!"

Randall closed the cover on the box and handed it to one of the constables. The other one was on the phone to the bartender at the Kilt and Jeans trying to get a description of the girl Matt had left there with.

Randall followed Scott to his room. Scott felt more help than just the local police would be needed to find Matt, and he passed Randall Chief Inspector Bradshaw's card with his phone number at Scotland Yard. Randall placed the call to Bradshaw on his cell phone.

While Randall was trying to reach the chief inspector, Scott picked up the room phone to tell the Royal and Ancient he'd withdraw. He took a deep breath before touching the numbers for the R and A tournament director, but Randall stopped him with a shout before Scott got connected. Bradshaw's request to speak with Scott was urgent, and the Turnberry Security Chief handed his cell to Scott.

Bradshaw's familiar clipped accent filled the earpieces. "The security chief brought me current on the message you received from your caddie's kidnappers. Have you withdrawn from the tournament?"

"No, but I was about to make a call to do it."

"Don't withdraw, Scott." Bradshaw said.

"I have to, Chief Inspector. Whoever did this could do worse if..."

Bradshaw interrupted him. "Scott, listen to me," he implored. "We have quite a bit of experience with this type of threat, and giving in to those people will not guarantee your caddie won't be harmed further."

"I've got to withdraw." Scott said. "I just can't take that chance."

"Scott, hear me out. Something we've been onto here at the Yard is just starting to reach critical mass. We've a strong lead on who's responsible for Matt's abduction. I'll put on a crew immediately to step up our effort relating to this investigation. How long before you have to tee off?"

Scott looked at his watch. "I have ninety minutes. Does this have anything to do with the feathery?" A thought that the feathery was *cursed* crossed Scott's mind.

"No, I'm sure it's a motive connected to gambling only. I'm asking you to put your call to the Royal and Ancient on hold. To withdraw right now would be the wrong move. I need a few minutes to pull some things together here that'll give you more justification to continue play. Give me thirty minutes to regroup with my people, and I'll ring you up after."

"I'll wait for your call, then" Scott said after a short pause, "before I withdraw."

***

Close to half an hour later, the musical tone on Randall Lyle's cell phone went off. He handed the phone to Scott. There was a delay before Bradshaw spoke. In the background, he could hear others offering information to Bradshaw.

Finally, the chief inspector said, "we've been working on a case that involves wagering on sporting events, and it's also tied to the Open. This has led us to those who kidnapped your caddie."

"Have you located Matt?"

"Yes, we know where he is and we're taking appropriate action for his safe release as we speak. We've an undercover agent planted with the gang that kidnapped him. Also, we received a phone call from Belfast. It seems the organizer of the abduction, one Malachy Gallagher, has given himself up. He's pin-pointed the location where your caddie is being held. I'll inform you of the progress when I know more, but I recommend you not withdraw. We feel Mr. Kemp's release is imminent. Go win the British Open." Bradshaw ended the call with, "Best of luck. I'll watch you on the replay tonight."

Some of Scott's anxiety lifted, but strong concern for Matt still lingered on after Bradshaw ended the call.

Randall Lyle broke into Scott's silence. "Scott, the media will come at this like piranhas, so let's keep the reason for Matt's absence secure. How about Matt is down with the flu and has a high temperature? Doctor wants him to stay in bed today."

"That might work. Thanks, Randal."

"You're going to need a caddie, Scott."

"I know. Got anyone in mind?"

"It's quite late to find one before your tee time, you know. Derrick might have someone. I'll ring him up him."

When Derrick Small entered the room, he offered a suggestion. "Would Douglas McEwan be alright?" I saw the young lad hanging around the putting green earlier."

Scott came away from his thoughts about Matt. "Isn't anyone else with more experience than Douglas available?"

"It's last minute, and all of the others are already taken." Derrick grinned. "Douglas was trained to caddie by the best...yours truly."

"Okay, I'll go with Douglas. I'll head for the range and meet him there. I've got another forty-five minutes before my tee time."

errick located Douglas and escorted him to the range. The boy was thrilled to caddie for Scott Beckman. Derrick calmed him down and gave him a stern lecture about keeping his remarks off the course. He then gave him a pat on the back, saying, "You'll do well, lad."

***

Scott hit only a few shots on the range before leaving for putting practice. The wind was blowing a gale and it was raining hard when he reached the practice green. The temperature had dropped, but the cashmere sweater under the top half of his rain suit held off the chill. Douglas tucked in two extra towels and made sure there was a sufficient supply of golf gloves in his bag for a wet and wild day. An experienced person adapted to doing so in the local weather could still manage an umbrella in the wind and Douglas showed that experience as he held one above Scott while he practiced putting. He would miss Matt's expertise, but Scott had some comfort in the belief that Douglas would know the course and how it played in the wind and rain.

On his way to the first tee, Scott spied Beth in the crowd and walked over to her. She was dressed for the weather in a light blue rain suit that was a compliment to her figure, and the color went well with that mass of jet-black curly hair.

"You've done so well. Keep it up, Scott," she said.

Douglas was standing behind Scott with the golf bag slung over his shoulder. "You have a new caddie. Where's Matt?" Beth asked.

Scott moved close to her and spoke very softly about the reason for Matt's absence.

"Oh shit, is this about the feathery?"

"No, it's about gambling on golf."

"Can I do anything to help?"

Scott thought about her offer for a few seconds. "Would you stand by the phone in my room and bring me any news about Matt? Call the head of security, Randal Lyle, to take you out on the course if you hear anything."

"I'll do that."

"Thanks. You can watch the Open on television there." Scott handed her his room key and headed for the first tee with a proud Douglas McEwan following close behind.

Despite the weather, a large gallery was surrounding the first tee. They were dressed in rain suits and carried large multicolored umbrellas. Scott's playing partner was Kuniaki Yamazaki from Japan, and he was alone in second place. Yamazaki had won a few tournaments in Japan and Australia, but had been on the U.S. tour two years without a top-ten finish. He was one of the few to make it to the Open in a regional qualification playoff. A multitude of fans who had made the trip from Japan were in the gallery, and a large group of Japanese press photographers were positioned near the ropes. If Yamazaki won the British Open, it would be the first major golf tournament won by a native of that golf-crazed nation. He bowed, smiled and said a few polite words in English to Scott.

When, Scott Beckman, the tournament leader, was introduced, a ripple of applause went around the first tee. He hit his drive. It was caught in a crosswind and deposited in a bunker on the right side, 284 yards out. Yamazaki's drive was a perfect three wood to the left side of the fairway, and a roar from the thickly populated Japanese crowd followed it. Scott made a bogie on the first hole and Yamazaki a par.

From there it didn't go well for Scott. When they reached the seventh tee, called *Roon the Ben*, Scott was three over par on the day and Yamazaki at even par, leading the tournament by two shots. The twosome of Yamazaki and Beckman were still in first and second place respectively because the wind kept the field playing in front of them from gaining any ground.

Douglas was doing a good job, and neither the caddie nor the weather could be blamed for Scott's play. Scott had played better on this same course in the same conditions during practice, but today his thoughts kept wandering to Matt, and the concentration needed for each shot and putt was absent.

Yamazaki's caddie was aware that Douglas was a novice. When Scott's shot reached the green of a par three, hole-high against the wind, the Japanese caddie approached Douglas before Yamazaki would select a club for his shot to the same green. His question was said in broken English. "What club your bag use for shot here?"

Douglas, at five-foot-five, pulled his body up to about five-foot-eight and frowned down at the Japanese caddie, saying, "It's against the rules to tell you that, so bug off."

Scott was within earshot of that exchange, and heard Douglas' rebuke. He smiled...his first of the day. Then his thoughts returned to more worry over the fate of his regular caddie.

B eth was watching play on the television in Scott's room when the phone rang. Several earlier callers were seeking news about Matt, and she thought this might be another one of those.

"Hello. Scott Beckman's room."

The voice on the other end asked, "Hey, who's this? This is Matt."

Beth snapped up in her chair and exclaimed, "Scott's caddie, Matt, Matt Kemp? Beth Sweeney here. Is it really you, Matt? Where are you?"

"It's me for sure, lass. I'm at a police station in Larne, Northern Ireland, about twenty miles north of Belfast."

"Are you okay?"

"Yeah, except for the mother of all two-beer hangovers and a missing gold earring that was not removed gently. Is Scott playing?" He asked.

"Yes, he's on the seventh hole, three over for the day."

"Good, I was afraid he might withdraw. Please tell him I'm okay, and I'm trying to get to Turnberry for tomorrow's round. Travel by sea is out. The ferries to Portpatrick have stopped running because of the bad weather, and there's no commercial flights to Scotland out of Belfast airport until around noon tomorrow."

"Hold on a minute, Matt, I'm getting the security head, Lyle, on my cell phone."

Beth told Randal Lyle about Matt's problem after locating him near the green on the ninth hole. He radioed the local police with the information that Matt was located and then caught up to Bob Bray on his way to the 10th tee. He passed on the news about Matt, and mentioned his difficulty in returning to Turnberry. The pilot of Bray's Gulfstream was following Bob Bray behind the ropes. Bob approached him, and after a short conversation with the pilot, Bob came to the security golf cart and spoke to Randal.

"The pilot of our Gulfstream said he'll be there inside of two hours to pick up Matt. He wants Matt to get to the Belfast Airport private terminal as soon as possible. Even though commercial flights are grounded, he may be able to slip in. But the pilot doesn't want to hang around there long because the weather at Prestwick on return is going to get worse."

Lyle passed the plan on to Beth and she in turn to Matt who was still on the room phone. There was a pause from Matt and some talk in the background before he spoke. "The local police have volunteered to whisk me to the airport. I'll wait there for Bray's airplane."

"How did you get free, Matt?" Beth couldn't help asking.

"I got some help. I was released near here, and found a police station. Let Scott know what's happening." And then Matt added, "Tell him to make some birdies on the back nine. Okay? Thanks, I have to rush, bye."

Beth called Randal Lyle, and the security golf cart pulled up in front of the hotel lobby shortly after. He wiped the seat beside him with a dry towel and handed Beth a yellow slicker like the one he was wearing. Randal spoke into his hand-held radio, asking for the location of Scott Beckman on the course. The answer came back, and they drove off into the rain and wind toward the 8th tee.

***

Scott just made a par on the 7th hole and was walking to the 8th tee when he saw Randal and Beth drive toward him. He tried to prepare for what could be the worst news about Matt.

Beth beckoned Scott over to the golf cart and said breathlessly, "Matt's alright. I just finished talking with him."

Scott stood still and looked up at the gray sky for a moment before he asked her, "When will he be here?"

"He should be in Turnberry after you finish play."

"Not sooner?" Scott asked anxiously.

"Not likely. He may be delayed by the weather, but he'll be here to caddie tomorrow. His message for you was to make some birdies."

"I'll try. I feel a bit more like it now. Thanks, Beth. I'll see you after I finish."

After hitting a huge drive on the 8th hole, called Goat Fell, Scott walked off the tee feeling like a weight had been suddenly lifted from him. He birdied not only the 8th, but also the next two holes. And he rounded out the rest in par except at the 17th, Lang Whang, where he made an eagle three. Lang Whang was becoming his favorite hole. When

Scott walked off the 18th green he still led the British Open on this third day, and one stroke better than Yamazaki.

Yamazaki bowed and shook Scott's hand. He said, "tomorrow, I'll play with you again." He turned and was escorted by Randal's men through the horde of Japanese cameramen clamoring to photograph the one who could well become their long awaited national hero.

After they signed their scorecards, the two players were escorted to the press tent. Scott had to field a few questions about his missing caddie. He was thankful the news of Matt's kidnapping hadn't leaked. When he left the press tent the wind gusts were even stronger than during play, and the rain was heavier. He decided not to practice in such harsh conditions. He was also anxious to get the latest on Matt, so he headed straight for the locker room.

***

Scott entered the locker room after signing some autographs. Douglas McEwan had finished cleaning his clubs and was hanging up some foul-weather gear to dry. He paid Douglas in cash, and the lad was taken aback by the two 100 pound notes put in his hand.

"Thanks for taking Matt's place, Douglas. You did a great job in this weather. Looks like Matt will be back on the bag tomorrow...Oh, and by the way, you were right on standing up to Yamazaki's caddie when he asked you about the club I'd hit on that par three."

Douglas was all smiles. "It was nothing, Mr. Beckman. I'll be following you tomorrow after doing some ferreting on Arran." He tried to hand Scott back the money. "I'd rather play a round with you after the Open instead of being paid so much."

"How about if I do both?" Scott said.

The smile on Douglas' face broadened, and his exclamation was an American origination he'd picked up recently. "Awesome!"

Scott left the locker room and walked up the hill to the hotel. The rain had let up some, but the wind was still howling through the Linksland. The forecast for tomorrow was worse than today. It would be another day to test a player's shot-making skills in severe weather...a day only a gannet would love.

When he entered his room he was pleased to see Beth and thanked her for standing by the phone. Their kiss was a long one, ending a tumultuous day that had finished much better than it had begun.

***

The Gulfstream V landed at Prestwick at seven in the evening with Matt on board. He called Scott from the Kilt and Jeans just as Scott was finishing dinner in the hotel dining room with Beth. The waiter handed Scott a phone.

"Hey, Scott, have you seen my earring?" Matt said.

"The cops kept it for evidence, but I'll buy you a new one. You don't know how great it is to hear your voice. How are you?"

"Tired, and I have a sore place where my earlobe used to be. But I'll be okay in the morning. Bob Bray's pilot got me out of Belfast and into Prestwick through some really nasty weather. I was given a tetanus shot and some antibiotics at the clinic here. Hey, I heard you're leading it."

"Yeah, unbelievable. Everything started working on the back nine, but I need you to keep it going in tomorrow's weather. Tee time is one-thirty."

"I'll sleep in until ten and meet you in the locker room at eleven. Good night, dude."

42

Douglas McEwan was up and about early and cooking his breakfast porridge. After eating it, he pulled on his boots and buttoned his raincoat. The hood of the coat fit snugly over his red curly hair and its drawstring framed his freckled face. He quietly closed the door to the small cottage bordering the Turnberry courses and walked out into a gale-force wind partnered with hard-driving rain. He thought it would be a good day for ferreting out the rabbits thinking they'd hunker down in their burrows, away from the storm and the noise of the Open crowd.

He was excited about Scott's chance to win, and after he finished ferreting he looked forward to following Scott with his father. Could Mr. Beckman continue to handle the wind? His da often said, "nae wind… nae golf," and the earliest McEwans of St. Andrews had passed along those words through generations. Douglas wasn't sure he could ever live up to that phrase because he preferred to play when the wind wasn't blowing at him or his golf ball.

He fetched his ferret from the shed next to his house, and the animal seemed eager to get on with the hunt as he pulled hard at the leash. Douglas fed him a small lump of sugar and grabbed a burlap sack from a pile on the floor. He opened the shed door with the ferret under his arm and faced an onslaught of a hard-driving rain that stung at his face. The thrill of caddying for Scott the day before still lingered as he trudged toward the Arran course with the empty burlap sack over his shoulder.

***

Scott was finishing breakfast in his room when the phone rang. It was the chief inspector.

"I want to wish you the very best today." Bradshaw said.

"I've got my caddie back…thanks to you. What was that all about?"

"It was about the amount of money bet on you at high odds. The owner of Barkley's Betting Shops, Ian Barkley, was intent on your withdrawal from the Open. His object was to stop his potential losses in case you won."

"How did you get on to them and get Matt released?" Scott asked.

"Barkley was a person of interest in your feathery robbery. I cross-checked information on him with a Scotland Yard team working on gambling irregularities, and found out they had Barkley and his bodyguard, an ex-IRA operative, Malachy Gallagher, under surveillance. Most of Barkley's activity dealt with fixing horse racing and football, and he had a crew, inclusive of Gallagher, fixing jockeys and football players. But we're pretty sure this was the first time Barkley has tried to fix professional golf."

"How did you find Matt?"

"Well, this Gallagher chap called us from his mother's house in Belfast to give us the information on where they were holding Matt, and then he turned himself in. We have Gallagher in protective custody, since he's a key witness against Barkley. Because of his cooperation we're working on a reduced sentence for him, with the possibility of amnesty for his crimes when he was with the IRA."

"How did Scotland Yard surveillance people miss Matt's kidnapping from the Kilt and Jeans?"

"The Yard was watching race tracks and football pitches for Gallagher and his team to show. They hadn't linked Barkley's golf-fixing angle until your caddie's kidnapping came about. But we caught up to them in Northern Ireland when we got the tip from Gallagher. The rest of getting him free was left up to the undercover agent we had planted there."

"Why did they let Matt go?" Scott asked.

"The kidnappers who'd held your caddie in Larne, Northern Ireland, were ex-IRA whom Barkley had a hold over. He knew of their past deeds of carrying out terror bombings in London and other violence. Our mole, whom they trusted," Bradshaw continued, "convinced those holding Matt Kemp that he had information from other ex-IRA sources we were closing in on them...so they released Kemp and ran."

"Have you rounded up the bad guys?"

"Not quite, Scott, but we're doing so with the help of the Irish police."

"How about the feathery robbery and murder?" Scott asked.

"The others, who had a keen interest in bidding on the feathery, to include Carrabba, Barkley and Sarah Covington, have been cleared of any implication at this time. Arrests in Spain and New York have gathered up the killer and his accomplices. Their London connection, Mary Harding, is in custody."

"That's good news. Where's the feathery?"

"It's on my desk as we speak, and I'm admiring it. Of course I'm wearing latex gloves while examining it."

To Scott, it sounded like Bradshaw was eating while he spoke. "When will I get the feathery back?"

The mastication sounds continued while Bradshaw talked through them. "I'm admiring all three of those fascinating antiques on my desk as we speak." Said Bradshaw. "The feathery will be on the way to you at Turnberry shortly by special courier along with the bronze statuette and the McNair Journal. They're not needed for evidence. We have photos and a confession from the key conspirator, Mary Harding."

"Great work by you and Scotland Yard, Chief Inspector."

"Thanks, Scott. Now, concentrate on your game today. I'll be watching on the telly....Cheers."

***

Later, when Scott entered the locker room, Matt was busy rubbing down the grip on one of the golf clubs. Matt put it quickly in the bag and stood up to receive the bear hug he knew was coming. Scott's eyes misted over, and that embarrassed him until he noticed that his friend, since childhood, was leaking bigger drops.

Matt indicated the bandage on his ear. "Someone doesn't like Sherpas who wear a gold earring."

"It could've been worse if Bradshaw and Scotland Yard hadn't found you," Scott said.

***

When they reached the practice green, gusts of wind laden with rain were causing umbrellas to attempt flight, and the force of it sprung some inside-out, rendering them useless and soon candidates for a trash barrel toss. Scott wore two cashmere sweaters under his rain suit jacket and a wool watch cap stretched down over his ears to hide most of his blond hair. Matt had the golf bag ready for the weather and was intent on protecting the club grips from the wet and keeping Scott as dry as possible in these conditions.

At the putting green, Randal Lyle beckoned Matt over to the ropes. "Knowing what you've been through, lad, I wouldn't expect this storm to bother you much." Then with a smile he added, "I'd say, it's a good thing you're still on this side of the grass."

Scott's eyes met Matt's. Lyle's philosophical remark hit home to set the tone for their day. They would play this tournament, gladly breathing the cold-wet air and laughing at the wind.

43

The same player as yesterday joined Scott on this final day of the British Open. They shook hands. The rain and wind hadn't kept the entourage of Japanese media and Yamazaki fans away.

Spotting the McEwans behind the ropes, Scott hurried over to them. "Douglas, meet me at the pro shop tomorrow morning at ten o'clock with your dad and be ready to play a round of golf." He shook David McEwan's hand and gave Douglas a pat on the shoulder.

Douglas' face was flushed, and his joy may have let caution blow away in the wind. "I'll be there for sure," he said in a loud voice. "Now, just beat the pants off of this one." He pointed at Yamazaki.

Both their drives dropped into good positions on the fairway, but against the wind they were relatively short at 235 yards. Golf shots in the strong gusts were truly laughable. Downwind, wedges were being used where eight irons would be the normal choice and against the wind it was the opposite mode in club selection. Scott was having a problem with his putts. A gust seemed to hit just as the putter head was going toward the ball. Matt reminded him to widen his stance for more stability and better balance in the wind.

When they reached the 9th, Bruce's Castle, Yamazaki had tied Scott for the lead. The 9th tee was perched out on a rocky cliff, with a long drop to waves crashing below. Scott looked out toward the water and saw the gannets in a diving-feeding frenzy. The wind was at the player's backs. Scott had the honors after making his second birdie of the round on the 8th. It was time to use a driver to tee off instead of a conservative two or three iron. Scott had those two drivers in his bag…one with a face angle of eight degrees and the other with ten. He pulled the ten degree driver out of he golf bag. The added loft on the face would launch the ball high to ride the wind, and the driver's longer shaft would create more swing speed at impact than an iron or a three-wood.

Scott's driver caught the ball perfectly and it flew off the tee, riding the gale as it soared high above a stone cairn 200 yards out in the middle of the fairway. It came to rest almost another 200 yards from that marker.

"Awesome! Could be on the green," Matt said.

Yamazaki didn't want any part of Scott's high altitude game. He selected a one iron for a low trajectory that put him in the fairway 270 yards out.

Scott's ball ended up 390 yards from the 9th tee and 30 yards from the green.

Scott and Yamazaki made birdies and were both still tied for the lead. The leader board showed no movement upward by the rest of the field playing in front of them, and no players were on the course in back of Beckman and Yamazake who were the last to tee off.

Scott was up by one stroke over Japan's pride after the 16th, *Wee Burn*. The 17th, *Lang Whang*, had been Scott's best played hole in the tournament. He'd twice made eagles there. Today, the wind was crossing right to left. He thought, *If I aim at the bunker on the right with my drive, the wind will bring the ball back to the fairway and drop it short of another bunker on the left side.*

Scott followed his plan, and his three-iron drive landed close to the prescribed spot, but too far away to make the green on his second shot in the dangerous crosswind. His safe second shot lay-up set him up for a pitching wedge third that came to rest fifteen feet from the cup. But he missed his birdie putt. The Japanese was away and sunk his for a par. Scott had a 4-foot putt for par, but just as he placed the ball in front of his marker, a blast of wind moved it ten inches to his right. The marker was still in place, and it was a reflex act when he picked the ball up and moved it back to the marker.

Matt warned, "No, don't!" But it came too late.

Yamazaki was watching Scott's next move. If Scott would putt from where he replaced the ball behind the marker he'd be penalized two strokes. When he realized Scott wasn't going to putt from that spot, he called the rule infraction just as Scott was about to call it on himself. Yamazake said, "now you must play ball from where it rests after it moved by wind. One-stroke penalty for you for picking ball up."

Matt nodded and shrugged his shoulders. A nearby R and A official was summoned to the green and confirmed the rule called by Yamazaki. Scott replaced the ball on the spot where the Japanese agreed the gust moved it to, and his anger caused him to miss the five-footer and score a bogie for the hole. With the one-stroke penalty added, it was a two-stroke swing in Yamazaki's favor. He was one stroke up on Scott with only the 18th hole left to play.

They walked off the green. Scott was shattered by his mistake. The excitement among the Japanese crowd was now near pandemonium. Matt waited for the noise to die down before he took Scott aside near the water jug on the eighteenth tee.

"Okay, Scott, put it behind you and play this hole aggressively," Matt said.

Scott took in a large pull of air. "I blew it and feel stupid for not reacting to the rule and calling it before Yamazake."

Matt put his hand on his friend's shoulder. "Don't be. Half the pros on tour don't know that rule. Let's play eighteen and forget rule number eighteen dash two."

Scott muttered, "Smart ass caddie." They both smiled and some of their tension eased.

Yamazaki's three-wood drive split the fairway and landed 282 yards from the tee. The Japanese in the gallery voiced their approval and their hero's grin smacked with a premature taste of victory.

Scott tried to put the disaster on 17 out of his mind and focused on what he had to do. He stood behind his teed ball, looking down the fairway and thought, *Par four, slight dogleg right, 430 yards to the green; need a three to get in a playoff...if Yamazaki makes four. I've got to hit driver here. An iron won't get it done.* He hesitated and looked toward the crowd for a moment where Douglas McEwan was gesturing with his arm pointing down the fairway with a signal that meant Scott's drive had to be a boomer in order to tuck a second shot in close to the pin for the birdie putt. But the player and his regular caddie already knew that.

Matt handed Scott the 10-degree driver. The wind was crossing the fairway right to left, as on 17, but a safe shot here was out of the question. He set up for a fade that would cut the dogleg, hoping the fading ball would be held back by the crosswind so it wouldn't go too far right and end up in the rough composed of high heather.

Scott swung, and his Linksking driver head contacted the Titleist Pro V1x at 123 miles per hour with every bit of its trampoline effect kicking in. The ball streaked off the tee, took the cut at the dogleg and landed center fairway only 68 yards from the flag. It was a monster drive of 372 yards. Scott's relatively small following emitted most of the cheering heard around the 18th tee. The Japanese entourage was silent.

Yamazaki walked up to his ball. It was 90 yards behind Scott's and 158 yards from the pin.

Matt whispered to Scott, "Yamazaki is thinking he needs a three to win it. He'll try to stick it in close, but if he's just a little long, he'll catch the downslope and be looking at a twenty-footer."

Yamazaki's high eight-iron shot looked like it was headed for the flag all the way, and in the bleachers a premature roar was emitted from his large home-island crowd. Then came a chorus of deep guttural groans an instant after the ball scooted beyond the flag. And without enough backspin it rolled slowly down the sloped green toward a collection area, coming to rest 17 feet from the cup.

Matt handed Scott his lob wedge and some advice. "I want you to visualize this shot landing past the stick about four feet, and the backspin provided by the lob wedge should bring the ball away from the slope that grabbed Yamazaki's ball. You'll have a short putt to make a play-off."

Scott gripped the club. The most important shot of his life would be made with a golf club given to him by Sandy McNair. *Was it an omen?* He stood behind the ball for a few seconds, envisioning the shot Matt suggested. After three practice swings, he was ready. The 60-degree lob wedge made good contact as the ball was pinched between club edge and turf. It flew high, spun rapidly counter-clockwise, then started down on a line to the right of the flag. Scott held his follow-through while watching the wind bring the ball left. It landed a little beyond the flag, and what he saw next was like a slow motion dream. The golf ball seemed to stop for a second before the backspin initiated by the grooves in the wedge brought it toward the hole, where it disappeared.

A tremendous roar rose from the thousands surrounding the 18th. The volume and duration of the din meant only one thing…Scott's slow-motion dream shot was real. His ball was in the cup for a two, and Yamazaki would have to sink his putt for a play-off.

Scott kissed the shaft of the lob wedge on the spot where his name was inscribed. He then looked up at the cloudy sky and gave his thanks to Sandy McNair.

The massive walking gallery rushed to stake out their position around the green. It took a number of Randal Lyle's finest to escort the players there where a loud ovation welcomed them. Scott retrieved his ball from the cup and held it high, initiating another loud burst of cheering from the gallery as an acknowledgment for his eagle.

It was five minutes before the crowd settled down. Yamazaki took his time, and he stared at the hole from every angle. His caddie stood behind him and gave his opinion of the proper line for the putt to travel. There was an animated discussion between them about the break. Scott stood off to the side beside Matt with arms folded. The crowd was hushed.

Yamazaki stared at the hole for the last time and drew back his putter blade. A smooth swing of the club brought its face square to the ball and contact was made. The gallery was quiet until that inevitable loud and premature prediction heard at each golf event was exclaimed: "IT'S IN THE HOLE!" The ball was rolling ten inches away and looking good when a minuscule jump to the right spoiled that wrong prediction by the fan when a spike mark altered the ball's course ever so slightly to make it pass over the right edge of the cup and stop three inches beyond.

A moan of disappointment came from Yamazaki's countrymen as he dropped to his knees and stayed there for a long time. After a while he stood up slowly, and Japan's hope walked up to the ball and tapped it in for a par, and a second place finish in the British Open. Polite applause followed the tap in, and Japanese fan and media disappointment permeated the air over Turnberry.

Matt confirmed Scott's stunned realization when he met him with a hug that lifted his friend off the green. "Scott, we just won the British Open."

Scott shook hands with Yamazaki and his caddie.

Kuniaki Yamazaki patted Scott on the back while smiling and said, "perhaps we meet again at the Masters."

"Yes, we'll both be there, Kuniaki." Scott said, knowing they'd qualified for the Masters based on their Open finish.

Then Scott was off the green, headed for the scorer's building where he would carefully check a scorecard that included a penalty stroke and an eagle.

Beth Sweeney, Randal Lyle, Mark Breen of Linksking, Derrick Small, Bob Bray, Claudio and both McEwans formed a corridor of congratulations on the way to the official's building. Scott walked through the row of friends receiving a mixture of exuberant high fives, hugs and handshakes.

A helicopter passed low over the course. Scott's pent-up emotion of the last two days came to the surface when he thought of his father. Tears welled up and a few of them spilled onto Beth's rain suit as he held her close.

***

After the scorecards were checked and signed, Beckman and Yamazaki were escorted to the presentation ceremony. Scott inhaled deeply before looking up at a mostly gray sky just starting to show a little blue out by the dark granite outline of Ailsa Craig. The island had escaped from the clouds to once more dominate the western horizon.

The official engraver inscribed SCOTT BECKMAN on the Claret Jug immediately after Yamazaki missed the putt on the 18th. The Royal and Ancient would retain the original Claret Jug with the names of all the Open Championship winners since 1872 engraved on it. A replica of the trophy was presented to Scott along with the winner's check in pounds sterling...equivalent to $1,567,000. Scott accepted the trophy and the check with a short speech thanking his caddie, and then mentioned Sandy McNair, followed by others who'd helped him to get there.

Scott's acceptance speech was almost finished when he spied the red head of Douglas bobbing around for a better view among the adults. Scott said, "I'd also like to mention a Turnberry boy who did a great job pinch-hitting for my regular caddie. He's standing over there, and his name is Douglas McEwan." He pointed to Douglas. The television cameras and audio pick-up devices of four major networks swung toward him. When they settled on the lad, 78 million viewers could hear his high-pitched voice.

"That was nothing, Mr. Beckman. The best part was you beat the pants off all the others against wagering odds of two hundred to one."

The crowd chuckled and they were most likely joined by a world full of TV viewers doing the same.

44

On the way to the hotel with Beth, Scott met Sarah Covington. She offered Scott her congratulations after he handed her a check for $20,000 to pay the penalty for taking the feathery out of the auction.

"Thank you again for the reduction," Scott said.

"Beth is a good negotiator. Are you coming to Portpatrick tonight?" Sarah asked.

"No, but I'll be there tomorrow evening. I've got commitments with the press and other business tomorrow. And I'm planning to squeeze in the round of golf I promised the McEwan boy."

"You must really love the game to play the day after such a grueling win," Sarah said. "Beth is welcome to come with me to Portpatrick this evening instead of hanging around Turnberry all day tomorrow. I'm off to London mid-afternoon and she'll be alone only a few hours before you arrive. The weather is going to be lovely and she'll enjoy the beach. I'm leaving for Portpatrick directly."

Scott looked at Beth for her approval and said, "you'll miss the celebration they've planned."

"That's okay, Scott. We'll have our celebration in Portpatrick. I'll go by the hotel, pack my things and go with Sarah."

Scott started to escort them toward the car-park when Sarah put her hand on his arm and stopped walking. "I've confirmed the feathery has been recovered. Do you have it in your possession?"

Scott hesitated before he answered her. "Yeah, it's locked up in the Turnberry Hotel safe with the bronze statuette."

"Oh, I'd love to see it, but don't bother now. When you get to London you'll let me have a peep."

"Sure, Sarah." Scott continued walking with Beth and Sarah to the lot where Sarah's BMW was parked. Sarah made another try to buy the feathery on the way there.

"It's not for sale, Sarah." Scott told her, once again.

When they reached the car, he kissed Beth goodbye and said, "later, in Portpatrick."

Beth looked up at him and the large brown eyes seemed to join with her smile. "Okay, until Portpatrick."

Sarah abruptly turned her back to them during their kiss and was quick to get in the BMW and start the engine. After Beth was in the passenger seat, Sarah drove quickly out of the parking lot toward the hotel lobby. The British Open champion stood alone for a moment thinking about Sarah's strong obsession to own the feathery, before he walked up the stairs to the function room..

***

The celebration was in full swing when the guest of honor arrived. All welcomed him into the Turnberry Hotel function room with cheers and more hugs or handshakes. Derrick Small had ordered a catered buffet as requested and funded by Scott. The Claret Jug was filled with champagne. First, Scott took a sip and raised it high in a toast before he passed the trophy around the room for all to partake.

Bob Bray offered his congratulations. He'd finished tied for seventh with more than enough prize money to finance a European vacation with his family. Mark Breen of Linksking requested a meeting with Scott before he returned to San Diego, wanting to discuss a European marketing thrust in light of Scott's Open win. They arranged to meet the next day. Mark was also keen on a playing a round of golf at Turnberry with the champ.

Douglas McEwan and his father joined the party, and Scott, to keep his promise to the boy, asked Derrick if ten in the morning would be okay for play on the Ailsa course. Even though Scott was feeling golfed out, he would play a fun round with Breen and Douglas.

"The course is officially closed tomorrow, but I'll make an exception for the Open Champion, only if I can join him," Derrick answered.

"You got it."

Douglas was a happy fourteen-year-old when he asked, "Could my dad join us Mr. Beckman?"

"Sure. You, Mark Breen and I will take on Matt, your dad and Derrick."

Matt was nearby and heard Scott setting up the match. "Okay, we stroke off the British Open Champ who has a handicap of plus five. That's five better than par on the Ailsa course, folks."

Scott was now ready to reward his caddie. "Without you, dude, I wouldn't have won this tournament." Scott handed Matt his personal check. "This will be good after I deposit the big one."

Matt protested after staring at the amount on the check. "Hey, that's way over the union wage for Sherpas. I'm looking at twenty-five percent here."

"I know, but you deserve it." Scott smiled. "Just consider the extra bucks for physical damages."

Matt's loud, "All right!" silenced the room. He reached in his pocket and withdrew a certified check from the Barkley Betting Shop. The check was written for a sum in British pounds sterling for the equivalent in U.S. currency of $176,130. "After what you told me about Barkley's legal problems, Scott, I figured I'd better collect this pronto at the Barkley Betting Shop in Prestwick. Claudio and I made a fast trip there."

A cheer filled the room and a good part of the Turnberry Hotel.

Derrick said it. "Scott, you're a bloody millionaire."

It all started to hit home with Scott. He thought, *In less than a year I've gone from being a broke dude to a rich one. And with the value of the feathery and bronze, it's even more. I could have done without the* shootings *over the feathery and Matt's kidnapping.*

Randal Lyle came forward to offer his congratulations and shook Scott's hand. "The Open Champion seems to be deep in thought."

"Yeah, I was thinking about Matt's kidnapping. The reason behind it was gambling on the Open." Scott rolled his eyes toward the ceiling. "This will be quite the flap for the PGA, USGA and Royal and Ancient to handle when it all gets out."

Randal agreed. "Yes, the righteous hypocrites in golf's hierarchy will be outraged, even though they've placed bets on golf at betting shops and casinos around the world."

***

The room started to empty as the caterer cleaned up the little food that remained. An overwhelming weariness suddenly came over Scott. The events of the week took their toll, and he was ready for some sleep. He entered his room and crashed, exhausted.

45

Scott was awakened by the phone at seven in the morning. It was his mother.

"Scott, I'm so proud of you. I watched the whole thing on television. That ace you made at the end was thrilling."

"Mom, it was an eagle. Ace is a tennis term, and a golf term for a hole-in-one, but thanks anyway."

"Whatever. I'm working on knowing more about golf and thinking of taking lessons. It's part of the therapy suggested by my psychiatrist, and it could be good for business."

"Quite a change, mom."

"Yes, I had a few hang-ups, Scott, but I'm working on them."

"They say admitting it is the first big step to recovering."

There was a pause. "And, Scott, you're a millionaire."

"Yeah, just like you, mom."

"Well, that's right. Oh, Scott, I hope we can start over and rebuild a good mother-son relationship."

"I'll try," Scott said.

"Good, congratulations. And, Scott, if you want to invest in some good California property, I can help. Goodnight, or is it good morning in Scotland?"

"It's morning here, mom. I'll be in California in a week or so. Bye."

Scott cradled the hotel phone and he lay in bed thinking about his mother. It was hard to forgive and forget her past attitude and bitterness toward him and his father about the game of golf, but he would work on it.

***

Scott was in the Turnberry Hotel restaurant at eight to meet Matt and Mark Breen for breakfast. Matt placed three Fleet Street tabloids on the table. The headline of one on the back sport page read: **YANK EAGLE SNATCHES OPEN WIN FROM JAPANESE.**

After Scott's interview with *Golf Magazine* they joined Derrick and the McEwans at the pro shop. Douglas and his father were ready for golf and bubbling with pride to be playing a round with Scott. The wind and rain had left Turnberry, and the clouds from the day before were starting to clear.

Scott shook hands with the McEwans. "I'm honored to play a round with the McEwans of Saint Andrew's." He turned toward Douglas. "Let's go, partner."

"I've been practicing and broke ninety on the Ailsa before the Open, Mr. Beckman. And I'm sure with all the strokes I'll get off you, we'll beat the pants off them," he said, nodding toward Matt, Breen and his father.

David McEwan looked to the sky with mock exasperation as if it was no use reprimanding his son any longer for his outspoken remarks. He shrugged and said, "it's in the lad's genes."

The course was empty and Derrick authorized their six-some to play the Ailsa—a little worse for wear because of the many divots made by a week of Open play. Using some of Douglas' 25 strokes, Scott, Douglas and Breen did beat the pants off Matt, Derrick and the elder McEwan.

***

When the round was finished, David McEwan invited them to his home, a short walk from the course. Derrick and Mark Breen played another nine holes instead of joining them.

After they settled into the McEwan parlor, the conversation turned to the McNair feathery. David McEwan showed more than general interest with a flurry of questions, until he asked, "May I have a look at your feathery?"

"Sure. It's in the hotel safe. I'll go get it." Scott started to get up.

"Nae, Scott, relax. I'll send the lad to fetch it."

Scott called the Turnberry Hotel desk to inform them, and Douglas dashed out of the house. He returned in fifteen minutes with the feathery. Scott opened the small wooden box and handed it to David McEwan. David reached in a desk drawer and put on a pair of latex gloves. He read the record scorecard and carefully lifted the feathery out of the box. He turned the ball slowly viewing the 78, HUGH and the pennyweight of 26. He stared at it for a couple of minutes before he placed the feathery back in the box with the scorecard. David handed the box back to Scott and excused himself. He left for another room in the house.

When David returned, he had an antique thorn wood driver in his grip. He handed the club to Scott and indicated writing on the head of it. Written there in black ink was the name HUGH, and under that, the number 78. The script on the club head was identical to that on the feathery. Scott was mesmerized by the familiar writing on the club and couldn't take his eyes off it.

David spoke to break the silence. "My ancestor from Saint Andrews, Douglas McEwan, made this club for Hugh McNair around 1849."

Scott again thought about the McNair journal he'd read. *The McEwan name matched the same name of McNair's caddie in the journal, and Douglas resembled that caddie's description there.* He asked David McEwan about the relationship.

"Oh, yes, that's definite, Scott, McNair's caddie during the record round was James McEwan, and James was the son of Douglas the club maker. We named our son after that Douglas."

Scott was still staring in astonishment at the markings on the club head and thinking about the McEwan lineage. "So, McNair used this club when he shot his 78 on the Old Course, right?"

"Aye, and it was a gift to James McEwan, his caddie back then. The legend of that record and this club have been passed down through generations of McEwans."

Scott gripped the club and waggled it a few times. "This driver is in great condition. It must be valuable." He handed the thorn wood driver back to David.

"Aye, John Hollbrooke offered me twelve-thousand pounds. I was tempted to accept that during hard times. I just couldn't part with it, but now I've decided to send it to its rightful place. It's going back to Saint Andrews, and will be on display there in the British Golf Museum."

Scott stared down at the feathery box on his lap for a long time.

Matt knew what his friend was contemplating. "Scott, are you sure? That ball is worth big bucks."

"So is the McEwan driver, Matt. I was just thinking about Sandy and how great it would be if the feathery returns to Saint Andrews to be on display in the museum along with the thorn wood driver that his great-grandfather used to set the record." Scott took another look at the feathery before he closed the box and said, "the feathery is going to Saint Andrews."

Matt shook his head. "You are one weird, rich dude."

Douglas asked his father, "Can I go to Saint Andrews with Mr. Beckman to take back the driving club?"

"If it would be all right with Mr. Beckman, it'd be all right with me, son."

Scott's thoughts were pulled away from St. Andrews in 1849. "Be glad to have him. It's only right that a McEwan present the club to the museum." He looked over at a very happy Douglas and added to his glee. "I'll pick you up on Thursday morning on my way back from Portpatrick. Bring your clubs, and we'll play the Old Course."

Scott and Matt got up to leave.

David McEwan shook Matt's hand and then held on to Scott's a moment longer. "You've earned the Claret Jug, Scott Beckman. You were a true gannet in our Turnberry weather. And now that you're going to donate the McNair feathery to Saint Andrews, you've preserved some history of a game you play so well." He released Scott's hand. "Sandy McNair would be quite proud of you."

46

S cott checked out of the hotel and drove the rented Land Rover down the long driveway and through the gate. The British Open crowd had left Turnberry, and the bustling golf-city of one week now returned to a quiet little village. It would stay that way until the Royal and Ancient designated its links to be the host venue for another Open. Scott was taking Matt to the Kilt and Jeans where Matt would meet Claudio and drive to Prestwick Airport for a flight to London. Claudio would go on to New York, but Matt had plans to stay in London for three days before flying to Santa Barbara.

As they turned onto the coast road, Matt said, "for you to set up the golf match for Douglas was a nice gesture. How many Open champions would do that the day after such a grueling event, and then invite the kid to play with you at Saint Andrews?"

"How about those two juvenile delinquents salvaged by Sandy at El Camino, Matt? When you and I were around Douglas' age we fantasized about playing with major tournament winners on British Open courses. I wanted to give the reality of that to the kid."

"I understand. What now, champ?" Matt picked up the Claret Jug trophy from the seat between them and looked at it admiringly.

"I've been thinking about the *what now*," answered Scott. "I'll take a few weeks off before playing the next tournament." He looked over at Matt. "Okay with you?"

"Yeah, I'll hang out in Santa Barbara and wait for you there. We can map out the schedule then. One tournament for sure will be the Masters in April where you can seek reality out of another childhood fantasy."

Scott smiled at Matt's remark and had pleasant thoughts about his British Open win qualifying him for the Masters. He asked Matt, "Why the three day lay-over in London?"

"It's part of that long story I mentioned to you in Santa Barbara before Q-School."

"You mean about getting fired by Sarah Covington. What else?"

"I was into a relationship with another player at the time I caddied for Sarah. Her name is Jennifer Lawton. Sarah had a kinda fear about her caddie fraternizing with the opposition, and she fired me."

"Wow! Sarah drops what she doesn't want and goes after what she does with a vengeance. But isn't...?"

Matt interrupted him. "It's complicated, Scott. Jennifer has been messed up by being around possessive women on the tour since she was sixteen. She's working her way out of it, and I think I can help. She was in love with me once. It can happen again. So, that's why I'm stopping over in London, dude."

PORTPATRICK

47

After dropping Matt at the Kilt and Jeans, Scott drove toward Portpatrick, on the very southern tip of Scotland. He would be late arriving there because of the meeting with Mark Breen to kick off the European promotion of Linksking clubs. And there was a photo shoot for advertising Linksking clubs in a golf magazine with too many retakes. Anyway, he'd make it to Portpatrick before dark.

Scott looked out through the Land Rover's passenger side window at the few clouds left over from yesterday's storm. Whitecaps were scampering about out on the Firth of Clyde and the Ailsa Craig loomed up on the western skyline. The gannets resting in the nooks and crannies on that rock of an island would wait until a storm came before returning to dive for fish in Turnberry Bay. He thought they wouldn't have long to wait if the local saying held true. He could see the Ailsa Craig now, so it must be *aboot to rain*. He again recalled Sandy telling him about that island, then a sad thought passed through him about Sandy not being there to see him win the Open.

He drove through the village center of Portpatrick and passed by its scenic little harbor. Fishing boats and pleasure craft were rocking at anchor in the gentle chop. Scott thought, *It could've been where the boat with Matt on board left from. Northern Ireland was only twenty-five miles from Portpatrick by sea, and the Blue Streak package with Matt's earring came from Portpatrick.*

Scott glanced at Sarah's direction notes on the seat beside him. They instructed a turn into a lane called Sand Niblick. Dunes banked the dead-end road on each side. A layer of drifted sand showed several tire tracks in the asphalt surface that came to an end near a lone cottage weathered to gray by sun and salt. The cottage was perched on a bluff, high above the beach and, in front of it, a breeze from the sea was blowing the dune grass in billowing waves.

A deep slice in a dune served as a crude driveway, and Scott pulled in between walls of red sand. He got out of the Land Rover and walked up slate steps to a deck that wrapped all the way around the cottage.

"Hello, Beth," he shouted. There wasn't any answer to his call. A knock on the door also went unheeded. He walked around the porch to a point where it faced the open sea and searched for her down a long stretch of sand. She was far down the beach looking out to sea and seemed transfixed by the beauty of a magnificent sunset painting the storm cloud residue a soft red. He hurried toward her, and when he was about halfway there, she saw him approaching, and in her bare feet with sandals in hand ran along the hard sea-washed sand to meet him. When they met Scott pulled her toward him and encircled her body with both his arms.

The sun was finishing its drop into the sea as they hurried along the beach and up a spiral steel staircase to the deck. They entered the cottage and closed the door on a horizon that soon faded from red to pink. And a short time later the sky darkened and became coupled with the same dark blue of the sea.

***

Scott could smell bacon frying when he awoke. He hurriedly got dressed and joined Beth in the kitchen where she'd just finished cooking breakfast. They kissed good morning and then sat at a table on a deck that overlooked the beach where gentle blue waves were turned to white as they broke on the sand below. They were quiet for some time, as if spellbound by the view...until Scott reached across the table for Beth's hand.

"It was nice of Sarah to let us have this place for a couple of days," he said.

"Yes, but I started to get the feeling that her hospitality might be all for the feathery." When Scott's look from across the table was quizzical, she expanded on that notion. "After we left Turnberry, Sarah talked to me a lot about how she would love to have the feathery in her collection. I think she was trying to enlist my help in getting it."

Again, Scott had that vision of the empty slot for the McNair feathery in the display case at Sarah's gallery. "I'm amazed, Beth, at how obsessive these collectors can get. The guy from Sweden, Johncke, had hit-men kill in order to possess it."

"Is he in jail?" Beth asked.

"No, he died before that could happen. Johncke used a lady, Mary Harding, to orchestrate his obsession. According to Bradshaw, Mary's motivation was partly so she could afford to lavish gifts on the one she wanted to have a lesbian relationship with."

"All of this happened because of an antique golf ball?" Beth said. "Hard to even imagine."

Scott recalled Chief Inspector Bradshaw's dissertation on collector obsession when they had first met in London. At the time, he couldn't imagine anyone having such a fixation on his feathery. He was now a believer in Bradshaw's conception.

"Could you show me this feathery ball that's so craved by those collectors?" Beth asked.

"Oh, sure." He got up from the table and headed for the bedroom. Scott returned, opened the wooden box, and said, "here's the feathery."

Beth stared down at it for a minute before she asked, "Do you think others, like that Swede, will satisfy their craze and try to possess this old golf ball the same way he did?" Then those expressive eyes of hers showed fear. "Are you safe having the feathery in your possession, Scott?"

"Well, someone might try to snatch it again, Beth, but anyway it'll only be with me two more days."

"You're selling it for megabucks, then?"

"No, that's when we're taking it to a museum in Saint Andrews."

"We are?"

"Yeah, it's the right place for Sandy's feathery and the McNair family legacy to rest."

Beth left her chair and walked around the table. She was suddenly on Scott's lap with her arms around his neck. "You're just the guy I want to love."

Her kiss was long and strong until she finally broke away and took Scott's hand, leading him toward the bedroom.

***

They spent two blissful days in Portpatrick. The rare sunny, clear weather supported it all in and around the charming village. They walked the beach for miles, swam in the cold sea and dined on seafood and French wine in quaint village restaurants.

The evening before they were to leave to pick up Douglas in Turnberry and take the feathery to St. Andrews, Sarah phoned.

Scott answered. "Hey, thanks for the use of your cottage. It's great."

"I'm glad you're enjoying it." There was a pause. "Scott, I wish you'd reconsider my offer to buy the feathery. The reason I'm asking again is, Mario Carrabba is in London for another auction and he mentioned wanting the ball so badly he'd exceed any other offer for it. I wouldn't think you'd want Carrabba to own the feathery after your past experience with him."

"Sarah, I've decided to give the feathery to the British Golf Museum in Saint Andrews." It will be on loan there indefinitely so visitors can enjoy the McNair legacy. Please pass that information on to Carrabba and any others who are still interested in buying it."

Scott heard a deep sigh come over the phone line, and it seemed like a long while before Sarah gathered herself to speak again. "When will it be in the museum at Saint Andrews?"

"I'm leaving tomorrow morning, and I'll have it there in the early afternoon."

"You know, I'm disappointed. But at least no other collector will own it. Oh bye the bye, what time are you leaving in the morning. I have a cleaning lady I must contact to come to the cottage."

"We plan on being out of here around ten to make an appointment with the museum curator."

She abruptly hung up the phone after giving instructions to Scott on where to place the keys after locking the cottage doors.

48

A t ten in the morning they loaded their luggage into the Land Rover. The box with the feathery, the bronze statuette and the Claret Jug trophy were safely wrapped in laundry and placed in a gym-bag. Scott backed the Land Rover out of that slice in the sand dune driveway, and they started down the narrow stretch of road called Sand Niblick toward the one leading to the village of Portpatrick , and then north toward Turnberry.

"Scott, look out!" Beth screamed suddenly.

Blocking the road fifty yards in front of them was a large black vehicle. Scott thought it could be a BMW 700 series. It stretched across to the sand dune banks that lined the road on both sides. A large man in a black leather jacket was leaning against the driver-side door, and he was holding an automatic weapon pointed toward the oncoming Land Rover.

Scott slowed the Land Rover when it was about twenty-five yards away from the BMW. Then he made a fast decision based on recognizing the guy with the gun—Carrabba's so-called chauffeur, Rocco. Scott yelled at Beth to scrunch down behind the dashboard. He was hoping the car's engine would stop any rounds headed her way. He accelerated the Land Rover and headed straight at the BMW and Rocco.

Rocco raised the gun to his shoulder and fired at the same time he jumped to avoid being crushed against the BMW by the speeding Land Rover. The leap spoiled his aim. The two rounds made a thud somewhere against the car's body just as Scott wrenched the steering wheel hard right to miss the BMW. The Land Rover plowed up the sand dune bank between Sand Niblick Road and the sea. At the top of the dune the vehicle's four wheels spun until they grabbed enough traction to slither down the soft-sand and find solid purchase on the beach below. The 300 horsepower engine with all-wheel drive was the right vehicle at the right time. They made it to the water's edge, and raced toward the village of Portpatrick along a beach hardened by the breaking waves of an earlier high tide.

Beth popped up from under the dash, looked anxiously behind them and saw that Rocco's BMW wasn't in pursuit. She turned to Scott. "If anything bad happens to your golf game, Scott, you might apply for a job in Hollywood as a stunt driver." Beth buckled her seatbelt before she continued, "It's dangerous hanging out with you. What was that all about?"

Scott explained the Rocco connection to Carrabba and the feathery in a few words. Before he turned left and drove up a boat ramp into the village of Portpatrick he wondered how Rocco knew where they were and when they'd be leaving the cottage. The answer came at him in one word...*Sarah*!

They looked up to see a police helicopter heading in the direction of Sarah's cottage. On the road several cruisers were racing in that same direction with lights flashing and sirens blaring. Scott asked the first person they came across for directions to the police station. When they arrived at the station they rush inside and told their story to the dispatcher on duty.

The burly uniformed officer sitting behind the desk said, "a chap by the name of Rocco Vitale was under surveillance, as ordered by Scotland Yard Chief Inspector Bradshaw and—" "What happened to the surveillance?" Beth interrupted. "We were shot at by that guy."

The dispatcher blushed with embarrassment before he answered. "Vitale slipped the man tailing him early this morning in Glasgow, but when gun shots were heard out at Sand Niblick our police responded in force by vehicle and helicopter. They're out there now, as we speak."

Just then a coded message came over a radio speaker somewhere nearby. After the message was complete, the dispatcher said, "they have Rocco Vitale down on the ground and in handcuffs."

After they left the police station Scott looked the Land Rover over for bullet holes before he headed for Sand Niblick Road. He found two holes in the hood that didn't appear to be lethal to any of the vehicle's working parts.

On the way out to Sand Niblick, Beth said, "my parents and friends will find this story hard to believe." When Scott gave her a puzzled look, she continued. "I've been dashed at breakneck speed by the British Open Champ next to the surf on a Scottish beach to escape a gunman, because someone wants to own an old golf ball."

"That story would be kind of hard to swallow if you left out the good parts, Beth."

She shook her head and laughed, and Scott joined her. It was a relief to laugh after the events of the last 30 minutes.

When they arrived out on Sand Niblick Road, Rocco was sitting in the back of one of the three cruisers. He glowered at them. His BMW was stuck at an angle about halfway up a sand embankment.

"Fortunate for us, Beth, that Rocco had the wrong car at the wrong time for his chase over the dune," Scott said.

The officer in charge called Scott over to him. "You're Scott Beckman. I recognize you from the Open. I've Chief Inspector Bradshaw on the line, and he'd like to speak with you." He handed Scott his cell phone.

"Hello Chief Inspector. What's this all about?"

Bradshaw's clipped accent came on. "We were alerted by Heathrow Immigration that Mario Carrabba and Rocco Vitale were in London. We tailed them to Sarah Covington's Gallery, then Carrabba left alone for Heathrow and a flight to the United States. Rocco drove him there and returned to the Covington Gallery. After being at Covington for an hour, he took a train to Glasgow. We alerted the police in Scotland, but they lost track of him until the gunshots at Portpatrick led to his capture.

"I suggest you ask Sarah Covington why she told Rocco we planned to leave her cottage at ten this morning for Saint Andrews, Chief Inspector." Scott said. "And while you're at it, you might ask Rocco who's payroll he's on now...Sarah's or Carrabbas'?"

There was a pause before Bradshaw said, "I've considered those points, Scott. I'll meet with Ms. Covington after the Scottish police interrogate Vitale and get back to you straight away with the results."

"By the way, Chief Inspector, the feathery is on the way to Saint Andrews where it'll reside in the British Golf Museum, safely guarded."

"I say, that is a good idea, and a commendable gesture on your part, Scott."

ST. ANDREWS

49

Four hours after leaving Portpatrick they were nearing St. Andrews, and Douglas showed his excitement by jabbering away until Scott's cell phone rang to interrupt him. It was Bradshaw.

"Rocco Vitale spilled the beans, as you American's say. When the Scottish arresting officers interrogated him he told them he had been hired for 200,000 pounds sterling by Sarah Covington to get the feathery away from you."

"Wow! I had a hunch Sarah was involved. But Rocco works for Carrabba. Was he involved in this?"

"No, Carrabba left for the United States after being told the feathery was going to the museum. Rocco stayed behind in London at Sarah's urging, and she hired him to do the dirty deed."

"Why did Rocco spill the beans?"

"He doesn't want to be extradited to the United States in fear of Mafia retaliation for deserting Carrabba. Evidently, the long arm of Carrabba's connections extend into the prison system there. So, a deal was made during Rocco's confession and his implication of Covington. He'll serve his time in Scotland, when convicted."

"Good work, Chief Inspector. What happens to Sarah?"

"She'll be tried and most likely convicted. She'll spend a long time in jail to pay for her feathery obsession. Have a good time playing the Old Course, Scott. Cheers."

After Scott touched the *end* button on his cell he thought again about Sarah's display that held the golf balls used by Beck, Geiberger and Duval. That empty slot inscribed with the name Hugh McNair would never be filled.

***

They arrived a half hour before their appointment with the British Golf Museum curator. Scott carried the box with the feathery inside, and Douglas carried the McEwan driver wrapped in bubble pack tucked under his arm. Beth walked along with them and commented on the historic atmosphere of the town of St. Andrews bordering the course. Scott and Douglas listened politely, but their attention was mainly on the mystique and tradition of the Old Course.

Scott checked their tee time and asked permission of the starter to walk out on the 18th fairway. He wanted to feel the Old Course's last hole as Hugh McNair might have during his record-breaking round…Also, he'd walk the same ground where Sandy learned his golf. The starter was so in awe when he recognized the British Open Champion he would've very well cleared the whole course if Scott had requested it. The first players out of the morning were only on the 16th hole, so the 18th was void of players. They headed out toward the 18th tee.

Scott stopped in the middle of the famous stone bridge over the Swilcan Burn "Douglas, this was where Arnold Palmer, Jack Nicklaus and others said good-bye to British Open competition," He said, then he whispered something in Douglas' ear that brought a devilish grin to the boy's freckled face.

They reached a place near the 18th tee and Scott paused again to speak to Douglas. "And this was about where McNair drove this feathery with the club you're holding on the day he scored a seventy-eight to break the record."

"I know *aboot* that, Mr. Beckman." Douglas took the box with the feathery in it from Scott and handed the ball to him. They both wore golf gloves on left hands that touched the feathery.

Scott's eyes zeroed in on the number 78 inscribed below the pennyweight 26 and the name, HUGH, on the bull hide cover. He squeezed it, again surprised at how hard this ball stuffed with feathers felt against his palm. Scott released his breath slowly and said, "just think, this ball was made more than one-hundred-fifty years ago in Hugh McNair's shop over there." He pointed to a group of buildings across the road next to the course. "McNair took it across the street to this old course of Saint Andrews and struck it only seventy-eight times. An outstanding score for the time he lived."

"Like today, Mr. Beckman, there would've been little wind and that's why Mr. McNair played his twenty-six pennyweight ball." Douglas was down on one knee pinching up an earthen tee. He handed the thorn wood driver to Scott and took the feathery from him. He held it a half-inch above an ant-hill-like pinch of turf, and then he adopted the dialect most Scots slip into if the issue before them is important. He said, "knock tha feathery oot wi' this McEwan club fer auld lang syne, Mr. Beckman."

Beth jumped quickly in between them. "Scott Beckman, don't even think about hitting that ball. That feathery and thorn wood driver are worth millions."

Scott's and Douglas' grins were wide.

The international lawyer thumped them each playfully on the arm with her fist saying, "You were both putting me on."

***

Later, they looked around the museum before their meeting with the curator. A niblick club used by Willie Park when he won the first British Open was on display in one glass case. Feathery balls made in the nineteenth century by Alan Robertson of St. Andrews were encased in another. Other feathery balls by Gourley and Alexander of Musselburgh and Marshall of Leith were there. One case held feathery balls made by Hugh McNair, but none of those were as famous as the one inside the box Scott carried. Douglas stood for a long time in front of a display of golf clubs made by his namesake and great-great-grandfather.

They met with the curator of the British Golf Museum. He'd prepared a display case to accept the McNair feathery and the McEwan thorn wood driver. It was appropriately inscribed:

WITH THIS McNAIR FEATHERY BALL AND McEWAN DRIVING CLUB HUGH McNAIR OF ST. ANDREWS SCORED A RECORD FOR THE TIME OF 78 ON THE OLD COURSE, JULY 8, 1849

EPILOGUE

AUGUSTA, GEORGIA

The Masters

The azaleas and dogwoods were blooming. It was a Sunday in April and the final round of the Masters. The green jacket was draped on a hanger in Butler Cabin waiting for last year's winner to assist the new champion slip his arms into its rayon-lined sleeves.

The last group to finish included Scott Beckman with his caddie, Matt Kemp, carrying his golf bag. They were walking down the 18th fairway on the Augusta National course approaching the green where Scott's golf ball rested 21 feet from the cup. If he sank the putt he'd win the Masters by one stroke.

Continuous cheering from the gallery accompanied their walk to the green. It came from those captivated by Scott's rise from obscurity to this opportunity for victory in his second major tournament.

Scott beckoned for his friend, following behind, to catch up and join him. Matt was wearing the loose-fitting white coveralls mandatory for all caddies at the Masters, and Scott wore the color-coordinated shirt and slacks prescribed by his clothing sponsor. A visor with the golf club manufacturer, Linksking's, logo on it captured most of Scott's blond hair.

Matt caught up and matched Scott's long stride. They made eye contact for a few seconds...then both flashed tension-relieving smiles. When Matt turned his head to speak, his dark red ponytail shifted from one shoulder to the other, exposing a scar where his left earlobe had once been. He had to raise his voice above the loud cheers of the gallery lining the 18th to be heard. "It wasn't all that easy getting here, Scott."

Scott nodded, then his sun-browned face straightened from smile to serious. "Yeah, you got that right, dude...some weird stuff came down on us along the way. "Could that lovely lady I saw you talking to behind the putting green ropes be Jennifer Lawton, the LPGA's rising star?"

"You got it. She's between tournaments and wanted to be here the final day."

"How's that working out?"

Matt's smile was wide. "It's working—it's working."

***

They approached the 18th green, and Scott prepared to stroke a putt that would win the green jacket, the money, and arguably, the most prestigious of the four major golf tournaments. His tanned face held an expression of concentration while he studied the path his putt would take to the hole. Matt handed him the ball after he cleaned it with a towel.

Scott squatted behind his marker and placed the ball carefully in front so the edge of the dime barely made contact. He lingered, hunched down behind the Titleist for a few seconds, looking first at the ball and then at the hole. He slid the marker back from the edge of the ball and dropped it into the right hand pocket of his slacks. He stalked the green around the ball, focusing on his objective…a steel cup four and one-quarter inches in diameter sunk in a hole, twenty-one feet away.

Matt bent down behind Scott and whispered his estimate on how much the ball would break on the way to the cup. Scott took his stance with knees slightly bent and his left eye directly over the brand name inscribed on the dimpled white cover. He traced the line to the hole, once, twice and then a third and last time…It was a phantom line only visible in his mind's eye. He heard the silence of the crowd around the green and took a deep breath, exhaling slowly. He was ready to putt.

The putter came back with both arms as one, hinged in a pendulum motion. His head was stone-solid-still as the milled steel face of the putter moved toward the ball, directed by muscle and memory. He calculated the speed of the putter at impact to roll the ball a distance of twenty-one feet. The putter and golf ball made contact. Scott's head remained still. Four seconds later he looked up slowly and saw the ball disappear. The roar of the crowd masked the grand sound a golf ball makes as it drops in the cup and rattles its way to the bottom.

Matt gave him a bear hug that lifted Scott off the green. The caddie whooped his praise. "Scott Beckman, you've just won the Masters! The green jacket is really yours."

The crowd parted to allow a lady to run toward him with her arms reaching out ready to hug. Her large brown eyes look up at his. Scott laughed…She cried…before she also laughed. Their victory embrace lived up to the expectations of those in the gallery and millions more watching on television. After receiving congratulations from the other players and caddies in his group, Scott headed on a path lined with cheering friends and fans toward the officials who would check his scorecard.

A Georgia state trooper allowed a large black man with hair as white as snow to step over the ropes in front of Scott. He laughed as he reached for Scott's hand. It was Kyle Ross, the San Diego detective who'd brought him to El Camino Country Club and Sandy McNair. Scott pulled Ross toward him and surrounded his neck with both arms. Ross' laugh was louder as tears began to well up in Scott's eyes.

When he reached the first step of the official's building, Diane Beckman came forward. She kissed her son on the cheek. "Congratulations on your win." She gestured toward the three men lurking behind her, wearing suits. "Scott, I want you to meet these gentlemen. They are real estate developers who are planning a golf course with up-scale housing outside of San Diego. They'd like to have you as an investor and to participate in the design of the course...Your Masters win could make this a lucrative project for both of us."

"Okay. mom. I'll meet with them as soon as I take care of business with my score card and the green jacket presentation." He climbed the steps and entered the official scorers room, thinking, *Wow, this is a big turn around. My mother's into golf projects.*

Made in the USA
Middletown, DE
05 November 2021